SAIL A JEWELLED SHIP

Jacintha den Hartogh was in love with Constantijn, a young wood-sculptor, but unbeknown to her, other plans were being made for her future. When her guardian, a Dutch shipwright, was invited to Sweden to help in the building of the *Wasa* Jacintha had to go with him. In Stockholm Jacintha met again Axel Halvarsen, who had already cast a shadow across her life, and circumstances forced her to strike a strange bargain with him amid the controversial build-up to the *Wasa*'s maiden voyage.

SAIL A JEWELLED SHIP

Rosalind Laker

A Lythway Book

CHIVERS PRESS
BATH

First published in Great Britain 1971
by
Robert Hale & Company
This Large Print edition published by
Chivers Press
by arrangement with
the author
1990

C150740655

ISBN 0 7451 1092 4

British Library Cataloguing in Publication Data

Laker, Rosalind, *1925–*
Sail a jewelled ship.
Rn: Barbara Kathleen Ovstedal   I. Title
823′.914 [F]

ISBN 0–7451–1092–4

For
my MOTHER

AUTHOR'S NOTE

On August 10th, 1628, the warship *Wasa*, pride of the Royal Swedish Fleet, built by Dutch shipwrights, sank on her maiden voyage. For 333 years she lay on the sea-bed until in 1961 she was raised up again to be housed in the *Wasa* Museum, Stockholm. Among the many objects salvaged was a carved caryatid in the form of a mermaid. It was the face of the mermaid that inspired this story.

R. L.

SAIL A JEWELLED SHIP

CHAPTER ONE

It was hard to leave the house where she had spent her childhood. It mattered not to Jacintha den Hartogh that it had always been a poor place, often with little food on the table, and a quilt too thin in goose feathers to keep her warm in bed on winter nights. Quietly she went from room to room on that last morning, saying farewell to the past with lingering glance and gentle touch, not realizing that she was listening for the echo of voices that she would never hear again.

Finally she came to the studio, and entered, closing the door behind her. There stood her father's brushes in a row of jars along the shelf. She went across to them, and put up her hand to run her palm over the soft tips. It had been her task to keep them clean and always ready for his use. On the workbench at her side lay his palette, worn to a glossy polish where his thumb had held it. She ran her fingertips lightly over the dried paint. Vermilion. Indigo. Purple and ochre and Veronese green. How often she had ground the pigments that he used for his impasto, pounding away with the old stained pestle and the wooden bowl, and then carefully adding the white lead that her sister, Lysbeth, had made ready with the dammar in turpentine, according to instructions. It had always given Lysbeth pleasure to perform this small duty, standing at Jacintha's side with her dark head bent over her work, her wand-straight parting disappearing under her starched cap, and her winged brows knotted in concentration while the tip of her tongue peeped from one corner of her stubborn and somewhat petulant mouth.

Jacintha turned from the workbench, and her gaze went to the many canvases and panels stacked around the walls. Portraits. Landscapes. Biblical subjects. Street scenes. Not one could be kept by either herself or Lysbeth. All had to be sold, together with the contents of the house, to settle their father's many outstanding debts. Only some of his sketches, deemed to be of no value, which she and her sister had selected between them, were ready in a roll to be taken away. These, and a few personal possessions, as well as a small boat that lay moored in the nearby dyke, were all that they owned in the world.

Jacintha moved slowly round the room, pausing here and there to look once more at one painting and then another. There was a certain sad immobility to her finely-boned face with its high, rather prominent brow, straight nose, and rounded chin, but her grey-blue eyes held no glint of tears, not even when she came to a favourite portrait of her mother sewing, and there was no betraying quiver to the lovely

2

mouth with its deeply indented upper lip. She had shed her tears in full and in private, not daring to let Lysbeth see the violence and despair of her grief, for it was her role now to be comforter and protector, taking the place of beloved parents that had followed each other to the grave within the short space of eighteen months.

She came at last to the unfinished landscape that still stood propped on the easel. It showed a stretch of the wide Dutch countryside that was so familiar to her. Adriaen den Hartogh's evocative brush had captured that vaporous early morning moment when the sun's brilliance was caught by canal and wet sail and thick dew, and the sky over distant Delft held the delicate pallor comparable only to the innermost depths of a cream marbled tulip.

People were gathering outside the house. She did not have to glance through the latticed windows to know they were there. She could hear the murmur of their voices, and the scrape of restless clogs. Those who had loved and respected Adriaen den Hartogh would not be present. They had given him credit time and time again, sharing his delight when the sale of a painting to a passing traveller, or the arrival of payment from an agent in Amsterdam, had enabled him to slap his guilders down on their counters, together with a large order that invariably put him in their debt again. To them

3

the book was closed, and they mourned his passing. But there were others who felt cheated by his death, having ever harried him, and they were determined that whatever was left must be turned into cash or taken in kind.

A sudden thundering by an authoritative fist on the street door went booming through the house. Immediately there came a creak of boards in the room above as Lysbeth, who had been lying weeping on the bed, sprang up in alarm. Swiftly Jacintha went from the studio, and hurried with a swirling of her russet wool skirts to the foot of the stairs.

'Come down, Lysbeth. It's time to leave,' she called quietly. Then she waited until Lysbeth appeared before going up two steps to meet her, and take her by the hand. The young girl's face was swollen and tear-blotched, but she was dressed ready for departure, and her appearance was neat and tidy. The knocking came again, even more demanding than before. The two sisters looked at each other wordlessly. Then Jacintha swung about, and opened the door wide.

'Good day, Juffrouw den Hartogh.' The bailiff, who stood there under the lintel, was massive-shouldered and big-bellied, and he held a stout stick horizontally in both hands, pressing it against the thighs of his set apart legs, as though prepared to deal smartly with any resistance to public entry that might be offered by any person in the house.

Jacintha stood on one side, drawing Lysbeth with her. 'Come in, Heer Boreel. We are alone here, my sister and I. Everything in the house is in order, and nothing has been removed.'

He gave a bull-like thrust of his head as he peered into the hall. Then with a grunt and a nod he stepped inside. It was like a signal to all those waiting to move forward, and they crowded in, jostling together, already arguing about their dues, and not casting a glance in the direction of the two girls forced to stand pressed back against the wall.

When there was a chance to move again, Jacintha took her cloak from a peg, picked up one bundle that held their few clothes, which she handed to Lysbeth, and another that was heavier and quite bulky, containing provisions for their journey, she took herself. Then putting an arm about Lysbeth's shoulders she hurried her almost at a run from the house, not giving the girl a chance to take any backward glances.

Along the village street they went, and then followed the grassy path that led down to the dyke. There a small cluster of women awaited them, some with babies in their arms, others with toddlers clinging to their skirts. Jacintha slowed her pace, greatly touched that so many should have come to bid them farewell, but Lysbeth ran forward to fling herself with a sob into the arms of the blacksmith's wife, Vrouw Vesser, who had been a good friend to their mother during her long illness.

'There, Lysbeth,' the woman said soothingly, holding the girl's head against her ample breasts. 'Do not weep, child. Another home waits you in Amsterdam.'

'But I want to stay here!' Lysbeth sobbed desolately.

'It was your father's wish that you and your sister should seek out your mother's brother. Remember that he made Jacintha swear to it. You girls have no other living relative. It is only right that your own should take you in.'

'Uncle Jurriaen does not want us! I know it!' Lysbeth cried wildly. 'Or else he would have answered Jacintha's letter!'

Vrouw Vesser's eyes, clouding with concern, met Jacintha's gaze over the girl's head. 'Have you heard nothing?' she asked.

'Not a word,' Jacintha answered, 'but he may well have moved on to another address. That I shall find out when we get there. It's many years since my parents left Amsterdam, and they never corresponded with him.'

'It could be impossible to trace him!'

Jacintha, who was trying to keep this fear at bay, both from herself and Lysbeth, dismissed the possibility with a show of lightheartedness that she did not feel. 'I'm sure that problem won't arise. My father said that Uncle Jurriaen inherited the family home, and so even if it has changed hands there must surely be someone living in it who will know of its former owner, and where he might be found.'

'But—' Vrouw Vesser checked her words. The possibility of Jurriaen Haaring being deceased was not to be voiced in the face of Jacintha's glance that dared her to utter it. And after all, the woman reminded herself, Lysbeth was fifteen, Jacintha two years older, and both girls were better equipped to find work, should they find themselves without shelter in Amsterdam, than many others left to fend for themselves. Someone would employ them. If not, there were always the orphanages where they could work for bed and board. They would not starve, or be left on the streets.

Nevertheless the blacksmith's wife did not feel easy in her mind. With misgivings she watched the two girls step into their little flat-bottomed sailing-boat with its painted scroll-work and slatted thwarts. There was only a canvas cover tucked away in the forepeak under the tiny bow-deck to give them any shelter from the rain and some protection from the damp chill of the nights, and she was glad that she had put a blanket there for them. All the other women, now clustering around with last-minute good wishes for the journey, had each found some small gift to bring, ranging from a freshly baked loaf to a pair of warm stockings, and a shawl. She thanked God that it was summertime, and although the weather was capricious the girls should manage to sail the dykes and canals all the way to Amsterdam without too much discomfort.

When their gifts and bundles had been stowed away under the canvas, Lysbeth took the tiller while Jacintha ran up the loose-footed, rust-coloured sail. It flapped as it received the wind blowing across the flat countryside, and then curved like a petal as the boat drew away from the bank, and left arrow-ripples dancing away in its wake along the greenish water.

The women and children on the bank waved for a while, and then the group broke up and dispersed. Only Vrouw Vesser still stood there when Lysbeth turned for one last glimpse of home before the trees and a bend in the dyke took it from her sight.

After a while Jacintha was pleased to see that Lysbeth's spirits had lifted a little. Both girls enjoyed sailing, and knew how to handle their uncomplicated boat. There was enough wind to send them skimming along comfortably. Farmhouses, windmills, and thatched cottages, somewhat sparsely set about, went sliding by, and on all sides the lush meadowland stretched away to melt into the hazy distance.

'I wonder what Uncle Jurriaen will be like?' Lysbeth said suddenly. Now that the terrible break with the past was finally over she was allowing herself to think tentatively about the future for the first time.

'Papa was too ill to tell me much about him—in fact, I think he really knew very little indeed. He did ramble so much at the end that it was difficult to catch when he was lucid. But he did mention ships in connection with Uncle Jurriaen.'

'Could he have meant that our uncle went to sea?' Lysbeth asked soberly.

Jacintha's expression was guarded, not wanting to make her sister despondent. 'That thought has occurred to me, but in that case we must expect that he has a wife and family settled in his home. Papa said it was a grand residence with many rooms.'

'I'll not care to live on anyone's charity,' Lysbeth remarked strongly, lifting her sharp little chin. 'I declare I've had my fill of that in the past.'

As soon as Lysbeth had been old enough to understand why there were always tradesmen badgering her father for money, she had resented the way of life to which they had been subject. She accepted that an artist not fortunate enough to have large works commissioned must live from hand to mouth, but she had never been as close to her father as Jacintha, inclining more towards her mother, and held it against him that he was not able to give her the pretty things for which she craved,

9

especially as she grew to young womanhood, and became aware that her poor clothes did nothing to help her dark, brooding looks.

Strangely her father had always seemed to find beauty in her countenance, although in her opinion that was no compliment, for she always considered his vision to be quite distorted, irritated that instead of seeking wealthy patrons he should spend his time in painting plain, ordinary people going about their daily work at home and in the street, or dragging in some passing beggar to make a portrait of the man's raddled careworn face. She had never forgiven him for capturing her sulkiness on canvas when she had sat for him one day against her will, and at each subsequent sitting he had deliberately needled her in order to keep that mood upon her features. It had always seemed an added misfortune in her life that she should have inherited his passionate looks and straight black hair while Jacintha's face was moulded as finely as their mother's had been, with a honey-coloured hair that fell in the same luxuriant waves to rest in flat curls the size of bracelets on her shoulders.

'We can contribute to our keep, Lysbeth,' Jacintha said, replying to her sister's acid comment, and knowing what lay behind it. 'Not with money—we have none except the few coins in my purse, and those we may have to spend if we don't find Uncle Jurriaen or his family immediately we get to Amsterdam. But we can both cook and clean house. If there are small children we can teach them how to read and write, and even to draw and paint. And although I don't consider myself to be a professional seamstress, I could always turn my hand to that, and make up gowns for any lady in the house. I shall make all this quite clear to Uncle Jurriaen from the start.'

'It's strange to think that until a month ago we didn't even know we had an uncle in Amsterdam,' Lysbeth said ruminatively, 'and if Papa had not succumbed to that terrible fever we might never have known.'

That was certainly true, Jacintha thought, and remembered with sadness the fear in Adriaen den Hartogh's eyes when he had realized that he was dying, a fear not for himself, but for his daughters whom he was to leave penniless and unprotected. 'Go to your mother's brother, Jurriaen Haaring, in Amsterdam,' he gasped, wheezing heavily. 'He lives in your grandfather's house, and cannot refuse to take you in. It will not be through love, Jacintha, but through a sense of duty, and that you must accept submissively, and be thankful. Do you mark what I say?' Then she had tried to soothe him, seeing that his distress and agitation were making his fever rise, but he had gripped her wrist with a strength that had surprised her, and made her swear that she

11

would do as he wished. Then he had lain back exhausted against the pillows. Not long afterwards the fever had laid such a fiery hold upon him that he had muttered incoherently until death finally claimed him.

Her parents had had a good marriage. They had loved and quarrelled and buffeted each other with a lusty passion that had made no concession to convention, and from babyhood their daughters had been swept into that whirlpool existence that had taken no heed of the clock, material comforts, or the opinions of others. But Adriaen and Cornelia den Hartogh had civilised their young by speaking French to them for days on end, seen to it that they knew how to read and use a pen by the age of five, and encouraged both of them to seek through an enquiring mind the truth of all things divine.

That Lysbeth had hankered after a more mundane routine, rebelling against her parents' inability to conform, had been known by Jacintha for a long time, and she was convinced that in some strange way her sister's unpredictable moods stemmed from a certain basic insecurity that was not entirely due to the oscillation of their fortunes. Many times as a young child Jacintha herself had experienced the feeling of being shut out by the secret looks and soft words that passed between her parents, but she had learnt to accept that she was only an incidental part of their unique relationship.

But not Lysbeth. She demanded attention, and went to any lengths to get it, which resulted in displays of temper, insolence, tears, and—by contrast—swift embraces that reflected the warm loving depths that were also there in the girl's complex nature. And now Jacintha could not help wondering if Lysbeth really would settle to an organized existence, and adapt herself to the clockwork precision of a well-run household after so many years of unrestricted freedom. But that remained to be seen and in the meantime the two or three days' journey lay ahead, and that was enough to think about at the moment.

They slept that first night in a barn, which stood near the spot where they had tied up. It was no hardship, offering more comfortable accommodation than the boards of their boat, and the hay still held its sweet summer scents, being newly gathered. In the morning they washed in a nearby stream, and then ate sparingly of the food that they had brought with them.

It was after noon, and Jacintha was at the tiller, when they sailed into Delft. Both girls had visited it twice before, although on the first occasion Lysbeth had been too young to remember it. It seemed a very large town to them, its canals busy with boats and barges, and the narrow cobbled streets lined with tall, gable-roofed houses, the latticed windows holding bright spangles of sunlight.

'Oh, do let's spend a little time here!' Lysbeth implored, her head turning first one way and then the other as she watched the activity all around them. Jacintha hesitated, wondering if it were wise to delay, but the town was full of tempting sights and sounds. Then deciding that an hour or two could not possibly go amiss she kept an eye open for a suitable mooring.

They went sailing past the shop where Jacintha remembered her father buying oil and turpentine and other supplies. Soon after came the inn where once he and her mother had had some kind of celebration dinner. That had been when Lysbeth was still a baby, but Jacintha, although she had never known the reason for her parents' high spirits on that particular day, could still picture it in her mind's eye. Perhaps Adriaen den Hartogh had sold a painting, or had a portrait commissioned; but whatever the reason he and his wife had laughed, looked at each other with lovers' eyes, and allowed Jacintha to drink some wine. It had made her sleepy, and when she awoke their little boat was still far from home, and on the bank of the canal her parents were lying in each other's arms, deep in the flowery grass.

Near the centre of the town Jacintha steered into a quiet backwater away from the mainstream of traffic where old warehouses cast dark shadows deep into the still water. They discussed the risk of leaving their possessions in the boat, and decided that although it was nominal, the small wharf being utterly deserted and apparently disused, they would only leave the food and the roll of drawings, which were of no value to anyone but themselves. Their bundle of clothing could not be risked, and they arranged to take turns in carrying it as they set off on their little excursion, very conscious that it looked for all the world like a vast pudding ready for the pot.

They soon found themselves in the market-place. There they wandered around the stalls and booths, trying to ignore the mouth-watering fragrances of caramel and sugary sweetmeats and hot gingerbread, and moved on past the stacks of cheese and mounds of wet fish to where more delicate objects, brought back to Holland by merchants returning from the East, were displayed in a scarlet and gold glitter of lacquered boxes, rich brocades and gauzes, and jewelled trinkets of all kinds. Lysbeth could not be moved from this array until a fanfare of trumpets on the far side of the square caught everyone's attention. A group of tumblers, clad in suits of pink and yellow, was already limbering up for a display on a flagged terrace that made an excellent stage against a background formed by the façades of two tall houses separated by a narrow passage giving a glimpse of a courtyard and workshop beyond.

'Let's get right to the front!' Lysbeth cried excitedly, and pushed her way through the crowd without ceremony. Jacintha, hampered by the bundle, followed her, and they secured a good viewpoint by the steps leading to the terrace.

Jacintha hoped the performance would be worth while as it was obvious that they would be jammed there until it ended as more and more people pressed forward. But after a few minutes her doubts about the entertainment value of the tumblers' antics were dispelled. They were extremely agile and talented, making themselves into everything from whirling wheels to human pyramids, bringing plenty of applause. Then came an exceptional feat, involving the balancing of all the men upon each other's shoulders, and they formed a great fan-shape as they slowly leaned outwards. The girls gasped their amazement, and gripped each other's hand in their excitement.

Then suddenly there came the echo of running footsteps coming from the courtyard beyond into the passage, and there hurtled into sight a black-haired youth with a taut and desperate face. Too late he saw the tumblers. His attempt to skid to a halt in time to save a collision was in vain, and he went crashing against the man forming the supporting pillar for the others. In a toppling of legs and arms and bodies the tumblers collapsed cursing and shouting on to the ground together, the youth went sprawling with them. But he was first to his feet, and without pause he dived like an arrow into the spectators, slicing a way through them. In the same moment an infuriated voice came booming from the courtyard after him.

'Stop him! Stop him! Stop that runaway!'

With one accord the crowd, annoyed at the disruption of the entertainment, turned about as many of the men present went charging off in pursuit. Jacintha was knocked aside, half lifted from her feet in the crush of movement, and the button on a man's coat caught in the cloth of her bundle, ripping a long diagonal tear in it. Out tumbled a number of things, including Lysbeth's tortoise-shell comb, and her own silver thimble, which went bouncing away amid a forest of feet.

'Save my thimble!' Jacintha cried frantically to Lysbeth, who had been dragged away from her in the mêlée, and she clutched together the torn pieces of the cloth to save losing anything more. Then to her dismay she saw a flash of silver as the thimble was kicked out of sight into a gutter, and at the same time a careless heel stepped on the tortoise-shell comb, snapping it in two. Just a few feet away her best neckerchief was being dragged underfoot in the dust.

Desperately she dug and thrust with her

17

elbows, trying to get enough room to recover their lost treasures, but it was another minute or more before the pressure eased and people spread out again, enabling Lysbeth, breathless and not a little frightened by the incident, to lend assistance.

By that time the chase had vanished from the market-square into the side streets, and the tumblers, who seemed to have suffered no hurt, turned away from watching it, grumbling between themselves, and they began to set to with some eye-catching cartwheels and hand-springs to recapture the attention of the crowd.

After some searching Jacintha found her thimble, and retrieved it from a gutter full of rubbish, only to find it badly squashed out of shape. 'Look at it!' she exclaimed unhappily, holding it out on the palm of her hand, having already commiserated with Lysbeth over the broken comb. With a sigh she slipped it into her pocket, and it was then that she discovered that her purse had gone. Her face went white as paper. 'Our money! Somebody has stolen it!'

There was nothing they could do. Almost anyone in that crush could have seized the chance to pick a pocket. Although they knew it was pointless they searched around on the ground, but the purse had vanished. Lysbeth looked at Jacintha with a very real fear in her eyes.

18

'We're penniless!' she said with a trembling mouth.

Jacintha, furiously blaming her own stupidity for not keeping a constant hold upon her purse, was determined that Lysbeth should not suffer through it. 'Do not worry, Lysbeth. We've plenty of food to last us to Amsterdam, and several days more,' she said reassuringly, and did not add that she intended to cut down her own share of the food to ensure that state of affairs.

But Lysbeth was thoroughly unnerved, and unconsciously put Jacintha's blackest dread into words as they hurried back along the way to the wharf. 'If we cannot find Uncle Jurriaen, then we'll be destitute in a city we do not know!'

'Then we'll live on the boat for a while, and it should be simple enough to find work,' Jacintha answered with a calmness that she did not feel. A new uneasiness had settled like a weight in her stomach. Suppose something had happened to the boat in their absence! How foolish she had been to leave something so precious and vital to their existence unguarded to take this unnecessary and disastrous jaunt into town!

Her pace quickened steadily as her anxiety increased, making Lysbeth break into a jog-trot to keep up with her. Finally she broke into a run, unable to bear the suspense any longer, and went darting ahead down a narrow alleyway and on to the wharf.

19

But the boat was safe, lying where they had left it, and in her relief Jacintha leaned for a few moments against a warehouse wall, flakes of dried paint from the old wood coming off on her clothes, while she let the wild thumping of her heart subside. She made up her mind that under no circumstances would she leave it again. Not even for the chance of sleeping in a warm hay-barn. From now on they must always bed down in the boat, and take turns to leave it. She flung down their tattered bundle as they stepped aboard.

'Push the bow out, Lysbeth,' she instructed, seizing the sweep and putting it out over the stern. Then as the boat drifted away from the slimy wall of the quay she sculled it skilfully out of the shadows towards the main canal, an expression of grim determination on her face.

CHAPTER TWO

It was not until they were far out of Delft, skimming along under sail again, that Jacintha felt the last shivers of tension ebb away. She had let Lysbeth take the tiller, while she put to rights as best she could the damage done in the market-place. Taking needle and thread she had stitched up the torn cloak, making a neat seam of the long rip in the cloth. She had rinsed the

20

dust from Lysbeth's broken comb, and leaned over the side of the boat to wash clean the trampled neckerchief as well as a couple of undershifts that had been kicked about on the dirty cobbles. By this time evening had come on, making the sun red and heavy in the sky.

She had just spread the garments out to dry when her attention was caught by a slight ripple of movement under the canvas cover in the forepeak. A rat had slipped aboard from the wharf! It was attacking their little store of food! Was there to be no end to the misfortunes of this day!

Swiftly she snatched up a boat-hook, which was the first weapon that came to hand, signalled to Lysbeth what she suspected, and advanced cautiously. Summoning up her courage she bent down to catch hold of a corner of the canvas. Then swiftly she hurled it away, and flung up her boat-hook to strike. Behind her at the tiller Lysbeth gave a squeal of astonishment.

There, lying curled up in the small cramped space, one precious, half-eaten loaf beside him, was the black-haired youth that they had last seen being pursued from the market-place. He stared up at Jacintha with fierce, golden-brown eyes, wary and challenging under brows thick and panther-black. His was a lean and bony face, hardening towards manhood, the nose forceful with flaring, sensitive nostrils, and the

21

mouth wide and sensual.

'Put that boat-hook down,' he instructed briefly. 'Otherwise I'll take it and throw it overboard.'

'This is our boat!' Jacintha fumed indignantly, still holding it high. 'You've no right to be on it!'

'I had to get away from Delft,' he answered in an off-hand way, and very slowly he started to move, almost experimentally, his long, spider limbs. But as he had feared, cramp laid hold on him, suddenly twisting his muscles in thigh and calf, and his face became distorted with agony as he jerked, and tried to stretch out his legs. 'God's wounds! Help me!'

He leaned over to massage his muscles frantically, but he was hampered by being unable to use his right hand, which was loosely wrapped about with a strip of linen that looked as though it had been torn from a shirt-tail. And Jacintha saw that for a few moments at least the intruder was completely in her power. She had only to strike a blow at his head to render him unconscious. Then at the next village she could hand him over to whoever had a cellar in which to confine him until the authorities from Delft arrived to take the matter in hand. But he did not look evil. Only young and bold and wholly vulnerable. The boat-hook quivered in her hands, but still she hesitated, abhorrence at performing such a physically violent deed

22

overcoming her natural anger.

'Don't stand there!' he implored again. 'Give my legs a few thumps with your fists!'

'Go on, Jacintha!' Lysbeth urged from the tiller. But whether it was an order to deal a knock-out blow, or give assistance, Jacintha was not sure.

Her face torn by indecision, she compromised by lowering the boat-hook, and then shaking it threateningly just a few inches from his nose. 'What crime did you commit in Delft? Are you thief or murderer?'

He shot her an impatient glance. 'Neither!' Then in pain and exasperation he wrenched the boat-hook from her grasp, and hurled it far away into the water. It fell with a loud splash just as the cramp curled him up again, and he writhed helplessly in its grip.

'Poor man!' Lysbeth cried. No question now where her sympathies lay. 'Come on Jacintha! You take the tiller! I'll help him!'

'Stay where you are, Lysbeth!' Jacintha ordered sharply, not turning, but, furious at the stranger's impertinent disposal of their property, she set her hands on her slender waist, and glared down at him with no show of pity for his discomfort. 'Tell me why you were being chased? What law had you broken? I insist on being told!'

'Only that of breaking my bondage to a master carver, who has barred me forever from

23

entering the Guild,' he groaned bitterly.

'Why? Are you such a bad carver?' she persisted.

'No!' he shouted. 'Delft will never see a better! But it's prison for me if I'm caught, and smashed fingers in the process! Knowing my master he'll not be content with half-measures!'

Jacintha suppressed a shudder. She knew how vindictive the punishment meted out to runaway apprentices could be. Although the compression of her lips signified that her disapproval of his being on the boat had not lessened in any way, she knelt down, whipped off his high boots, and with the palms of her hands she pressed back the toes of his stockinged feet as far and as hard as she could, bracing herself against the effort involved. He threshed about, a dank odour of the bilges rising from his clothes, and banged down his fists like a wrestler performing at a fair. But eventually her rough treatment had some effect, and a final sharp massaging of his calves enabled him first to sit, and then to stand up. He reeled over to rest the flat of his good hand against the mast, holding the other bandaged one free, his arm crooked, and glanced towards Lysbeth with a smile, showing his appreciation of the concern she had expressed before returning his attention to Jacintha.

'Thank you for your assistance, Juffrouw. I've never experienced such an agonizing cramp before. But I suppose it was to be expected after a great deal of running, and then being confined in such a small space for so long.'

He was even taller than she had realized, and his linen shirt with its wide collar hung soiled and sweat-stained from his shoulders. His full breeches, fastening below the knee, were of coarse blue cloth, and a matching jacket was still lying rolled up in the bow where he had used it for a pillow.

'You should have made your presence known without waiting for us to discover you,' Jacintha remarked acidly. She had risen to her feet again.

'My apologies, but the longer I remained hidden the better my chances of getting far away from Delft without being spotted by my master, and hauled back again. You could have set up a fine old hue and cry at the sight of me, for all I knew.'

'Of course we could!' Lysbeth interposed eagerly. 'You were not to know. I'm Lysbeth den Hartogh, and this is my sister, Jacintha.' She took one hand from the tiller, and gestured prettily towards Jacintha, who met steadily his golden-brown gaze that seemed to be taking in every small detail of her appearance. She became aware that wispy tendrils had escaped from the sweep of hair that she had caught back under her cap, and were hanging on each side of her face. And that somehow the ribbon

25

fastening of her bodice had loosened, and her brown linen apron was water-splashed by her wringing of laundry into the canal. She spoke quickly to break his penetrating stare. 'Who are you?'

'I'm Constantijn Verstrate,' he answered with equal brevity, almost as a rebuke to the sharp tone that she had used towards him.

'How did you find our boat?' Lysbeth asked eagerly, her expression one of open pleasure at his presence, which was proving so diverting. 'We saw how you sent the tumblers falling about your ears!'

'Did you indeed?' There was a throb of laughter in his voice as he spoke. 'I gave my pursuers the slip by doubling back on my tracks, and I had intended hiding somewhere in those old warehouses until I saw your boat tied up alongside. The canvas cover offered an excellent hiding place.' His eyes danced suddenly. 'I must admit that I intended to take it and sail out of Delft as soon as it became dark—but then to my astonishment you two girls came jumping into it, and off we went.' Then, recalling how he had watched proceedings through a crack in the canvas, he gave a shout of laughter, throwing his head back. 'You sculled right under the very bridge where my master was scanning the crowded ways on each side of the canal for some sign of me!'

26

Jacintha's face remained unsmiling, but Lysbeth giggled, and her hand, which had been careless on the tiller since her attention had been distracted by Constantijn, causing her to steer a somewhat erratic course, now swung them too close to the over-hanging of a tree.

'Look out!' Jacintha cried. 'To starboard!'

The branches went snapping against the sail, showering them with leaves, but Constantijn had already acted, and it was his hand that swung them out into the canal again, avoiding collision with the bank. 'You'd better let me take over for a while,' he said to Lysbeth, and would have seated himself beside her, the tiller between them, if Jacintha had not spoken sharply.

'No! Leave that to Lysbeth. I've something to say to you.'

He turned about, and came back to take a seat on a coil of rope, leaning his arms across his knees as he looked up at her. 'Well?'

She sat down on the thwart opposite him, her back very straight, her expression stony. 'That bread you ate was part of our supplies for our journey to Amsterdam. You'll have to pay for it, and for the privilege of being brought this far in our boat. There's also the replacement price of one boat-hook.'

'Jacintha!' Lysbeth breathed, astounded that her sister should speak out in such a mercenary manner, for all that they needed to replace the money that had been stolen.

His eyes flickered in surprise, but he shrugged amiably enough. 'Whatever you say.' He reached for his jacket in the bow, and took a leather draw-string pouch from a pocket. He tipped some coins on to the palm of his bandaged hand, which he held out to her. 'Take what is owing.'

She leaned forward, and picked out a few stuivers and a duiten. 'These will cover it. I have not cheated you.'

But he continued to proffer the rest of the coins. 'I'll gladly pay whatever you ask to travel as passenger with you all the way to Amsterdam. I've a friend there—a wood-carver like myself—who lives in St. Anthoiesbreestraat. His name is Dirck der Meer. He'll help me to find work.'

'But no one will employ a runaway apprentice,' she pointed out grimly.

'Not in any small Dutch town, I grant you,' he conceded, 'but I'll make up some tale, Dirck will back me up.'

'Your master could come looking for you,' she warned.

'Perhaps I'll change my name—' and here he stroked his chin '—and grow one of those fashionable beards such as gentlemen sprout! Sharp as an arrow-head!' There was a chuckle in his voice. 'Now will you take me to Amsterdam?'

She shook her head, refusing to be swayed. To become involved could lead to all sorts of trouble. She and Lysbeth might even be accused of helping to inveigle his escape. 'It's out of the question,' she stated implacably, and shot a fierce look at Lysbeth, daring her to speak up on his behalf, and saw that an appeal was bitten back.

But Constantijn made no further attempt at persuasion beyond a disappointed sigh as he returned the money to his purse, and she noticed again the swollen fingers that showed under the tattered binding.

'What happened to your hand?' she asked.

'I knocked it.'

'Is there anything broken?'

'I do not think so, but it is quite bruised.'

'Let me see.' Carefully she unwound the linen, and as the last of the wrapping fell away she took his hard, puffed hand between hers, and drew it on to her aproned lap. 'Try moving each of your fingers in turn.'

He obeyed, and each digit responded well enough.

'You've been quite fortunate,' she commented. Then she leaned over and dipped the linen strip into the cold water of the canal, and then squeezed the surplus out of it. 'How did it happen?'

He watched her as she began to bind up his hand very neatly. 'I was at work on a large

29

oaken panel that had been commissioned for a municipal hall. Master Koster—to whom I was apprenticed—flew in a terrible rage when he saw how I had carved the central panel, and struck out at me. I fell, hitting my hand.'

'What was the subject?'

'Paris awarding the apple.'

'Why did your master not approve of it?'

'It was my interpretation of Aphrodite. He said it ruined the whole work.'

'Did it?'

'No.' He sighed ruminatively. 'It was the best carving I've ever done.'

With some conceit he regretted that it had been lost to posterity, but it was a relief to be free of Master Koster at last. Now he was really on his own. He could not return home to Leyden even if he had wished it, for his mother had long since become subject to the tyranny of her second husband and would be afraid to let him into the house. Indeed, it had only been in the heat of honeymoon that she had managed to persuade his new stepfather that Constantijn should be apprenticed to a master carver and not taken away from school just to knead dough and sweep floors in the local baker's shop. Constantijn was grateful for her foresight and understanding, but she did no more for him. He would have welcomed letters from her during those first long months made wretched by homesickness, but she never wrote or came to see him. He concentrated on his work, determined to become a good craftsman, and his talent was a source of jealous astonishment to Master Koster, who had never had such a pupil on his hands before.

Two years went past, and the stilted style imposed upon Constantijn by his unimaginative master built up such frustration that his relationship with the elder man was ever strained, frequently exploding into violent displays of temper on both sides. Constantijn, wholly aware of the interdependence of vision and understanding in the interpretation of life in the sculpturing of wood, found release by staying on in the workshop long after the other pupils had left, working by rush-light, often missing the meagre supper that was dolloped out each evening, while he carved in rapt solitude a number of pieces both in relief and in the round.

It was one of these, the Angel Gabriel, that was spotted by a visiting Burgomaster from The Hague. He took the piece into his hands, and his expert eye observed the vibrant strength of the figure with its finely planed brow and splendid incisiveness of wing feathers and drapery. As a result he commissioned a table-settle, and for the first time Constantijn was allowed to work freely, creating his own designs for the four panels, taking as his theme four great naval battles. The credit and the praise went to Master Koster, but that had not mattered to Constantijn, who accepted the fact that pupil-carvers, until becoming full members of the guild, could not hope for individual recognition. Unfortunately there was no easing in the relationship between master and pupil, and their antagonism towards each other continued to smoulder and erupt like a rumbling volcano.

Other commissions followed in a flood. Constantijn's chisel and gouge brought forth religious works for churches, and a number of fine doors, panels, and balustrades for both municipal buildings and private residences. Master Koster raked in the guilders, and determined that Constantijn, who had been foolish enough to mention plans for setting up his own school within his hearing, should remain bonded to him indefinitely. Arranging this matter would not present any problem to Master Koster, who was a member of importance in the Guild hierarchy, and could see to it that Constantijn's application for membership was turned down time and time again.

It was inevitable that eventually matters should come to a head between pupil and master, but not in the way that either of them could have imagined. Constantijn had been left to work on three vast oaken panels, depicting the judgement of Paris, while Master Koster went away on business. Much of the carving had already been completed, and the three panels, set together, were clamped against one wall in the workshop, reaching from floor almost to ceiling height. It was the most important work that had been commissioned to date, and Mevrouw Koster, knowing that her husband was reluctant to absent himself during these final stages before its completion, offered to supervise and to report to him by letter. It was a neat excuse to avoid accompanying him, but he accepted it without question.

Constantijn was disturbed by her coming daily with her embroidery to sit and watch him at work. They were almost always alone as he was devoting himself to the final figure of Aphrodite, and the other apprentices were at work in another room. He was distracted by the rustle of her silken skirts, and the faint aroma of musk that hung about her. Every time his eyes slid in her direction, hers were always waiting, full of a veiled, dark promise that made him misjudge more than once the angle of mallet and chisel. She was an exceptionally handsome woman, tall and deep-bosomed. It was not long before she made a point of shooting the bolt home in the workshop door after she had entered and closed it behind her. Had Master Koster returned unexpected during any night he would have found his wife sleeping alone in their wide bed, her virtue beyond doubt.

Constantijn, to whom she had been an entirely new experience, paid her a reckless and gallant compliment. On the side panels Hera and Minerva drew back before the central figure of Aphrodite, who bore the unmistakable features of Mevrouw Koster.

Master Koster, returning from his travels, went straight to the workshop, a vigorous, corpulent figure in his black, sleeved cloak, wide-brimmed hat, and stick and gloves in hand. His bouncing tread as he entered denoted all was well, and he had gathered in the desired commissions that he had sought in The Hague and at Rotterdam. Constantijn was alone, perched on his high stool, and did not turn from his work.

Then Master Koster stopped dead, and stared at the panel where the sunlight beams, full of dust motes, were touching into additional splendour a face and form that were all too familiar to him. He gave a shuddering gasp. Constantijn glanced down over his shoulder with a frown, blinking a little as he always did when wrenched from the depths of concentration. With mild surprise he watched the congestion of his master's outraged features as a purple colour flooded into the florid cheeks that shook pendulously, for the man's whole body was a-quiver with shock.

'What have you done?' Master Koster roared, not yet suspecting his wife of infidelity, but

34

only aghast at the audacity of his pupil who had dared to commit her through such imaginings to public view. Then following up came the devastating impact of all that it meant. The panel could not be presented! The loss in goodwill and in financial terms was beyond reckoning! And rushing back came the memory of all the difficulties that had arisen over getting this superb wood all the way from France while half of Europe was involved in a war that seemed to have no sense or end to it. It was the final straw, and brought him near to madness in the brain-splitting rage that laid hold on him.

'You fool!' he bellowed, swaying to and fro on stamping feet, so consumed by passion that Constantijn swung about on the stool, convinced that the man was about to have an apoplectic fit. But as he thrust his gouge back into the work-pouch on his belt, and would have jumped down to the floor, Master Koster struck out with the head of his heavy cane and dealt him a blow that caught him off balance, and sent him reeling back off the stool, which went crashing with him. Its heavy legs thudded against the base of the panel, the force knocking a clamp free. Then the three whole sections of that vast piece of work swayed forwards, wrenching out the other clamps, and both men saw it toppling down towards them. Constantijn rolled away, and Master Koster flung himself back as the carving fell with a noise like thunder, cracking over the stool, and raising splintered edges sharp as dragons' teeth amid the clouds of dust that rose up from the floor, bouncing from the impact, only to gouge itself again before subsiding.

Constantijn, who had sprung to his feet, stood with one hand cupped around the other that he had injured in falling, staring in dazed horror at the ruination of his work. Then he was wrenched about as Master Koster grabbed great handfuls of his jacket and collar, bringing that purple-stained face close to his, tainted breath foul in his face.

'You'll pay for this, Constantijn Verstrate!' his master bawled as though demented. 'Not just with every guilder you're likely to make for the next twenty years, but you'll make good to me a hundredfold every hour that you've spent giving vent to your lustful thoughts!' The powerful hands were twisting tighter the bands about Constantijn's throat as the youth struggled to free himself, half-choked by the pressure.

'That was French oak! A fortune it cost to ship it here! Commissioned for the new Town Hall! Ruined! I'll see to it that you're kept out of the Guild if it's the last thing I do! I swear it! You'll stay bonded to me for the rest of your days!'

The noise of the falling carving had brought everyone in the household to the workshop at a run. Mevrouw Koster pushed her way through the gaping apprentices gathered in the doorway, one hand to her heaving breasts, her face stricken, her orange-tawny skirts making a sudden blaze of colour amid all the sombre woods. One glance at her expression would have been all that was needed to fill in the last details of the situation for Master Koster, but at that moment, in desperation, Constantijn had swung up his hand to cover the man's face and thrust it away, the ball of his palm jerking up the chin with a crack. Master Koster went reeling back, lost his balance, and fell sprawling.

'Quick, Constantijn!' the Mevrouw screamed. 'Run! Now! It's your only chance!' Then, as she saw that he hesitated, seemingly still appalled by all that had happened, she tore at him with frantic hands, transmitting her panic to him. 'Go! Go!'

He went, hurtling away, and Mevrouw Koster's slamming of the workshop door behind him did little to delay the chase that had followed him in full cry.

Now as Constantijn sat watching Jacintha making a sling for him out of her neckerchief he wondered how far Master Koster's arm could reach out to haul him back again. The sooner he lost himself in the city of Amsterdam the better.

'Lean forward,' Jacintha said. He obeyed, and she tied the sling in a way that kept his

37

hand high against his chest. She noticed that there were little yellow flecks, bright as gold-dust in his eyes, and his lashes were thick and dark and curled crisply. 'There!' She patted the sling into place. 'That should ease the aching.'

Then for the first time she smiled at him. Just a tiny curling of the corners of her mouth, but it stirred his already awakened interest. She was not beautiful, and lacked the striking, almost tempestuous allure of her sister's looks, but there was a wonderul formation of bones in her face that made the sculptor in him long to touch and to discover, and her hair was the colour of amber in the deepening light of the evening sky. He had the feeling that she was a girl who would always hold back something of herself, ever a little mysterious, wholly intriguing, making a man seek the heart of her as though for treasure trove deep beneath the sea.

'You look like one of Wallenstein's wounded soldiers,' Lysbeth declared, breaking into his thoughts. And he saw that Jacintha jerked her eyes away from him as though she in turn had been forming an opinion of the kind of person that he might prove to be.

'I do indeed,' he agreed, and his eyes followed Jacintha as she moved away from him, although he continued to address Lysbeth. 'Why are you and your sister on your way to Amsterdam? And why were you in Delft today?'

Lysbeth was only too eager to give him their story, and as he listened he continued to watch Jacintha's neat, precise movements as she set out some food for his supper.

'I'll pay for this,' he said, as she handed him his share.

She looked at him steadily, distress darkening her eyes. 'I'm sorry to appear so grudging in hospitality, but our provisions must last us indefinitely. As Lysbeth has told you, until we get to Amsterdam we have no idea what our future holds.'

'Jacintha's purse was stolen in the market-place today,' Lysbeth informed him. 'We lost all our money.' Then she went chattering on again, filling in all the details. Jacintha, who had divided what remained of the loaf between Constantijn and her sister, together with some cheese, now poured a small measure of ale from a flagon into two horn cups, which she placed within their reach.

'Aren't you eating, Jacintha?' Lysbeth asked, taking a bite.

'I'm not hungry,' Jacintha answered, and surreptitiously scraped up the crumbs in her lap to pop them into her mouth as she turned away. Then she saw that Constantijn's eyes were on her, and she flushed, seeing her words had not deceived him.

'Here,' he said. And broke his portion into

39

two, and handed half to her, his gaze holding hers.

'Thank you,' she whispered. And when they came to the next village along the canal she did not tell him to go ashore as she intended.

They sailed on through the rose and gold evening, and when a deserted windmill loomed large and black against the sky it was Constantijn who brought the boat alongside the jetty, and tied up. They went on land together, and their footprints left a trail in the mealy dust on the floors as they explored the windmill and peered at the dark, silent machinery. Constantijn found a pile of sacks that would have made a comfortable bed for the sisters, while he settled down elsewhere, but Jacintha refused to leave the boat unguarded, and would trust it to no one but herself.

Lysbeth grumbled about the hard boards as they lay down under the blanket that the blacksmith's wife had given them, and again about the cold, damp atmosphere as night descended. But eventually she was quiet, and then Jacintha, wearied by the day's events, slept too.

It was early when she awoke, but dawn had already brought another bright day, and a light mist sparkled over the ground. Lysbeth was not in the boat. Jacintha, alarmed, threw back the blanket, and scrambled to her feet. She flung a shawl about her shoulders as she climbed on to the jetty and ran along the boards, but they were damp, and she skidded, and fell to her knees. One clog dropped with a splash into the canal, but she did not stop, and went pounding on into the mill. There was nobody there, although the indented sacks showed where Constantijn had been sleeping. What had happened? Had he been traced and taken away? Had Lysbeth followed him?

'Lysbeth!' she called frantically, and her voice went echoing round and round the mill. She kicked off her remaining clog, which was hindering her, and she tore up a ladder, making it sway, to look out of the window across the countryside. Then she saw in the distance two figures coming back across the fields. In the stillness, broken only by the morning twittering of the birds, their voices and their laughter reached her faintly on the still air.

Her immediate reaction of relief that they were both safe was instantly overwhelmed by a searing jealousy that went burning through her with a force that made her shake. It was an emotion so entirely new to her that she was frightened and bewildered by it. In a desperate attempt to subdue it before Lysbeth and Constantijn drew near, she hurried back down to the ground floor, and darted back to the dyke. There she rescued her clog that had come to rest amid the weeds, and slipped it on. Then, struggling to regain her calm as she knelt

41

among the wild flowers on the bank, she washed her face, scooping up the cold water, splashing it against her burning cheeks. By the time she had combed her hair they had drawn near, and she saw that Constantijn had discarded the sling, which meant that the swelling of his hand must have subsided under the cold compress as she had expected.

He hailed her jubilantly. 'Come and see what we've brought for breakfast!' Still pinning on her cap, her elbows high, she went to see what they had found. Her face was quite composed. There was nothing in her expression to hint at the turmoil of emotion still seething within her.

They had taken a stone jug, which he had rinsed in a stream, and milked a grazing cow that Constantijn had spotted from the mill window. It came to light that Lysbeth had risen and gone towards the mill just as he was about to set off, and together they had raided the outskirts of a farm orchard on the way back again. The shared expedition seemed to have cemented their liking for each other, and as they drank the milk and ate the food fetched from the boat they laughed about various small incidents together, not realizing that they were creating an intimate little aura of friendship about themselves that was making Jacintha feel shut out, forcing her to cope afresh with the seething, untameable misery inside her.

She took one of the green apples that

Constantijn held out to her as breakfast ended, and bit into it. It was hard and green, but not too sour, and she went over to sit by herself on the mill steps while she ate it, one arm resting across her knees, and tried to rationalize her feelings, which were mixed with shame that she should let jealousy rise up against her own sister for the first time in their lives together.

It seemed to Jacintha that she had become too concerned with Constantijn, her whole body attuned and alert to every small action and movement that he made; the flicker of his lashes, his very breathing, the knotted muscles in his broad back when he pulled on the tackle to lower the lee-boards, the undulating line of his flexible mouth, and whole young male presence of him that had filled her eyes, her nostrils, and seemed to sing through her blood. When he had shared his food with her the previous evening their hands had touched, making her heart thump.

It would be a good thing now when they parted. It should be tomorrow evening, or early the next day when they would arrive in Amsterdam, and it was doubtful whether they would ever meet again. Just as she and Lysbeth had to make a fresh start in life, so did he, and their paths were destined to split apart.

'We'd better be getting on our way,' she said, standing up, and she tossed her apple core far into the long grass. Constantijn finished pouring what was left of the milk into a spare flagon to take along with them, and then he went ahead to clamber into the boat, and hold it steady for the girls to step aboard.

They made good progress that day. The weather was warm, the breeze sufficient, and they saw themselves perfectly reflected in the water as they sailed along. In spite of these conditions, far from favourable for fishing, Constantijn managed to catch a couple of sizeable trout, which they decided to cook for supper that evening. Lysbeth washed his shirt for him while he took a bathe over the side, and attached it to the mast to flutter dry. Later he sat for a long time carefully restoring to shape Jacintha's crushed thimble with the aid of a number of different gouges that he took from his work-pouch. Finally he held it out to her.

'That's splendid!' she said with gratitude. But when she reached for it his fingers closed about the thimble, making her glance at him in sharp surprise. He caught the unguarded fiery blaze before her lids lowered, but she rebuked him calmly enough. 'I'm in no mood to play forfeits.'

Then he let her take it. He had sensed right from early morning that her attitude towards him had changed. Her composed stillness, which had the effect of making everything else about her seem busy and confused, held a new element that he could not define. He was reminded of ice over the river in early spring when underneath the waters are wildly surging. If she had been deliberately playing out a line to him he could not have seized upon it more eagerly, and his eyes followed her as before.

That evening after they had eaten supper around a fire of twigs and bracken on the bank, Jacintha wandered off on her own. The grass was tall, misty with cow-parsley, hampering her skirts as though she waded through the sea. Presently she sank down and rolled over on to her back, and lay stretched out in the dark green shadows. Idly she plucked a buttercup, and lay twirling it, its bright gold reflected on the pale, luminous skin under her chin as she gazed upwards at the dusk-blue sky.

She heard him come looking for her, but did not move. The stems of the flowers and the tall grass stalks snapped before him as he pushed his way through. Then suddenly he saw her. He stood there with his feet apart, one on each side of her crossed ankles, staring down at her.

'Why did you not answer when I called?' he demanded in his strong, reliable voice.

She drew the flower through a loop of her finger and thumb, and answered him carelessly. 'It's peaceful here.'

'I was getting anxious.' His stare did not ease.

'Where's Lysbeth?' She made a little restless movement of her head as though to lessen the

45

pressure of his eyes, and threw the flower aside.

'Making up the bed on the boat. She's tired.'

'I'd better help.' She raised herself up on one elbow.

'Not yet.' He dropped slowly to his knees, sitting back on his heels for a moment. Then he leaned forward, set his hands heavily on her hips, and followed the line of her legs through the thickness of her skirts down to her ankles where the layers frilled out under his grasp. 'I love the shape of you, Jacintha,' he whispered reverently. 'The way you walk, move, stand—everything about you.'

Her heart began to pound in great, heavy throbs, and a strange languor took all power from her limbs as he moved to lie down at her side. He cupped the back of her skull in his hand, and with the other he gently explored with his fingertips the line of brow, chin and throat. Then his mouth took hers, opening up its warm, moist depths to her, initiating her into a way of kissing that added to the wonder of other delights as his searching touch moved on to discover the sweet, secret shapes of her body.

It was Lysbeth's voice, calling distantly, that finally made them draw apart, smiling, breathless, knowing that they loved each other. To her the sensation was wholly miraculous, unlike anything she had ever known or dreamed about, and as he drew her to her feet she felt as

46

though she were floating dreamily through some measure of slowed-down time. As she made her way with leisured, rising step back to the boat even her hair seemed to lift and drift about her face in silken spider strands. She looked back over her shoulder at him, and it floated between them like a veil.

She had forgotten her linen cap, which had fallen from her head, and he bent to pick it up, astounded at his longing to protect and cherish this girl who had brought a lifetime of herself into his arms for the short spell that they had spent in the grass together. Her innocence delighted him, making the tricks and wiles and erotic little games of Mevrouw Koster and her kind, for all they were pleasureable enough at the time, seem part of a world on which he had closed the door for ever. Nothing existed for him beyond this desirable creature, who—like a new, delicately-tuned, but as yet unplayed lute placed in his hands—was his to touch into a thousand exquisite melodies.

He put the cap to his lips, unashamed of his open joy, and tucked it into his shirt as he went hurrying to catch her up. Then hand in hand, kept speechless by the loving conversation of their eyes, they would have wandered right past the boat if Lysbeth had not called to them. She saw at once that love had come to them, and was glad.

Long after Lysbeth had fallen asleep Jacintha

and Constantijn sat in the bow talking over their plans for the morrow when they would reach Amsterdam. Jacintha had decided that it would be better if he did not accompany them to Uncle Jurriaen's house, as it might lead to dangerous questions about whence he came, and why he had journeyed with them. He must go straight to his friend's rooms in St. Anthoiesbreestraat, and there Jacintha could get in touch with him. Later she could introduce him to her uncle as a resident of Amsterdam, which he would be by that time, and—if fortune favoured him—one of the city's many wood-carvers. Whatever happened, nobody must know that he had ever set foot in Delft.

'You do not have to go to your uncle's home at all, Jacintha,' he argued, not for the first time during their discussion, and now he added the persuasion of kisses to his words, tightening his arms about her. 'Stay with me. I'll get work, and so could you. We would be together.'

But she drew back from him, an absorbed sense of purpose showing on her face, as though the proximity of Amsterdam had put all else momentarily from her mind. 'I gave my word to my father that I would carry out his wishes, and that nothing would deter me from that duty. I know that his fears were more for Lysbeth than for me. I must see her settled in Uncle Jurriaen's home before I can make any decision about my own life.'

He saw it was pointless to argue further, and tried to console himself with the thought that he would rather see her comfortably housed and well looked after than scrubbing doorsteps and floors for a pittance until he could afford to keep her. But then the realisation came home to them that when night fell again they would be separated by strange walls and unfamiliar surroundings as far apart from each other as if the whole of Holland lay between them. They did not have to put it into words, for both knew what the other was thinking as they sat curled up together, and they drew even closer in their rapt embrace as though seeking comfort against the thought, her arms round his neck, and their whispering lips within brushing distance.

'It will not be long to wait, Jacintha. Soon we'll be together for always.'

'Oh yes.' There was a look of unutterable love in her eyes, her face was entranced, her smile trembling. 'In the meantime we'll meet often. There's nothing to fear.'

'Why did you say that?' he asked after a moment's reflection. 'About fear, I mean?'

She lifted her brows. 'I don't know. And yet it was strange that I should have said it—I fear nothing now that we have found each other.'

They stayed there together all through the night, her sleeping head in the hollow of his shoulder, her cloak over them as cover. He lay

49

there listening to the swaying of the reeds as the breeze went rustling through them. It made a lonely sound. Like the sighing of parted lovers.

As though to seek reassurance he burrowed his face into the silken tumble of Jacintha's hair, inhaling her warmth. Only then did he sleep.

CHAPTER THREE

They sailed into Amsterdam the following day in the late forenoon, passing the old fever hospital, and the great windmill by the bridge, one of many lying on the bulwarks of the city. The sun had finally conquered the earlier showers, giving a hazy luminosity to the scene, and above the distant rooftops the bulbous and waisted church towers caught and held the dazzling rays.

The waters of the Amstel proved to be so busy that Constantijn took command, and steered their little craft expertly through the moving maze of fishing-boats, sail-boats, East Indiamen deep in the water with undischarged cargoes, small tubs and row-boats of every kind. There were many barges, bright with their scrolled patterns on bow and stern; some had canopies, taking people on outings, and others were loaded with grain, churns, and barrels of pickles and salted herrings. Once a finely ornamented boat with liveried oarsmen went swiftly past, and the looped-back curtains of crimson velvet gave them a fleeting glimpse of a lady in black with a large white ruff, stiff as a dinner-plate.

Jacintha and Lysbeth were so fascinated by all they saw that when Constantijn finally tied up in the shadow of a large tower, having followed directions shouted to him in answer to his enquiries, they were taken by surprise, and there was a last minute scurry to collect everything together.

'It should not take you more than seven or eight minutes to reach your uncle's house from here,' Constantijn said as all three of them stood on the path that ran alongside the canal. 'I'll wait at this spot until an hour has gone past. Then I'll know that all is well, and the door has not been shut against you.'

'I wish you were coming with us,' Lysbeth said dolefully, tucking the roll of her father's drawings under her arm. All her doubts were rising up again now that the meeting with the unknown Uncle Jurriaen had become imminent.

Constantijn looked at her with a smile. 'You know where to find me, and as it happens we'll not be a great distance apart after all.' Then he turned to Jacintha, and took her face between his hands. 'But I'll gladly accompany you and

51

see you safely there.'

Jacintha longed with all her heart for the moment of even so brief a parting to be delayed, but her fears for his safety were greater, and she shook her head. 'No, Constantijn. We must keep to our original plans. It is the only way.' But her mouth trembled under his kiss, and she clutched at him as he held her. Then resolutely she stepped back, and took the pudding-like bundle of their possessions from Lysbeth, and settled it firmly in the crook of her arm. 'Tomorrow,' she promised him. 'I'll come to the house in St. Anthoiesbreestraat tomorrow.'

'I'll not go from there until you come, Jacintha,' he replied fervently.

A last long lingering look of love passed between them. Then she turned about, taking Lysbeth by the hand, and the two sisters passed through a dank and stony archway with an echoing clatter of clogs into the street beyond.

It took them longer than they expected to cover the estimated distance from under the old tower where Constantijn had landed them to Uncle Jurriaen's address. At first Lysbeth had delayed progress, hanging back to stare in wonder after some finely-garbed lady and gentleman, or darting over to press her nose against the thick panes of any shop-window displaying wares that caught her eye. Then suddenly they found themselves faced with a detour. A new canal was being dug through that part of the city, and the resulting congestion of coaches, horses, pack-mules and pedestrians made the going difficult. Again and again they were forced to follow one curving way and then another until Jacintha realized that even if they retraced their steps to the boat the hour would be up before they reached it, and Constantijn would be gone, thinking that all was well. There was nothing for it, but to press on.

They came at last upon the ruin of a street where the earth-works of the new canal were crumbling a way through as men dug and shovelled, hauled on pulleys, and clanked about on boards making passageways through the sticky mud. Jacintha turned in appeal to one of the many clusters of spectators that hindered the way of others as they stood watching the work in progress.

'Could anyone tell me where to find Mynheer Jurriaen Haaring's house on St. Catharinastraat?'

Those that heard her turned to glance in her direction, most of them with a blank stare customary to those accosted by a stranger, although one or two showed mild amusement, which she soon understood.

'This was St. Catharinastraat.' It was a fisherman who had answered her, standing solid in his high sea boots, and he threw out a horny weathered hand towards the raw depths of the scored earth. 'Now it is to be part of the new

53

canal. All the houses that stood here came down months ago.'

At her side Lysbeth gave an indrawn gasp of dismay, but Jacintha spoke up again. 'The Haaring family had lived in that same house for several generations. Surely there must be some way of tracing them?'

There were shrugs as a few mumbled amongst themselves, and the fisherman took off his woolly cap, scratched his head, and pulled it on again. 'That presents quite a problem. This is not one of your country villages. Amsterdam is a large city, you know. Nigh on one hundred and fifty thousand folk live in it. What was the name again? Haaring? What profession or trade did the family follow?'

'I'm not sure,' Jacintha answered, feeling foolishly at a loss.

'Well, then.' The fisherman flapped his hands at his sides to express the futility of further effort, but then suddenly a thought struck him. 'Here! You might try asking at the Town Hall.'

She thanked him for the suggestion. Surely at the Town Hall some records of this evacuation would be kept? But time enough to start enquiries tomorrow.

'Come, Lysbeth,' she said eagerly. 'We'll find Constantijn now, and tell him what has happened. His friend will surely offer us accommodation for this night, and then in the morning we'll start our search afresh.'

'At least we know why Uncle Jurriaen didn't answer your letter,' Lysbeth remarked as they retraced their steps. 'Simply because he never received it!'

They found the house on St. Anthoiesbreestraat. It was within sight and sound of the wharves where the great ships docked, and they passed many foreign seamen on their way. The whole district was faintly exotic, and on one of the quays a cask had been dropped during unloading, sending clouds of fine brown spice wafting away on the wind, and its fragrance was everywhere.

A woman with wet soapy arms, hands red from hot water, answered the door to them with a scowl, and shook her head when they asked for Dirck der Meer.

'This is the second time within the hour I've been brought from my laundry work to answer enquiries after that young rogue,' she snapped with vigorous impatience. 'He's gone. Long ago. And do not ask me where, because I've no idea. If I had I'd be after him for the rent that was never paid!'

She made to close the door again, but Jacintha thrust her hand against it. 'Please! Just one moment! What of the young man who also enquired here? Where did he go?'

'God in Heaven knows, Juffrouw, but not I!' she rapped out. 'I've more to do with my time than to query casual callers about their business.' Then she slammed the door shut in their faces.

The two sisters looked at each other in complete comprehension of their ill fortune. 'We're alone, Jacintha,' Lysbeth said nervously. 'Constantijn has no idea where we are, and how can we find him?'

'Let's get back to the boat,' Jacintha said grimly. 'It's our only link.'

But when they went running back along the towpath under the tower walls they saw that the boat had gone.

*   *   *

Constantijn had left the tower far behind him, intent on steering a clear course through the traffic on the busy waterway, and was making his way to the nearest shipyard. He was confident that Jacintha and Lysbeth had been welcomed into their uncle's house, and would have no need of the boat for a little while. Their failure to return had cast him down, for secretly he had hoped that Jacintha would not be pleased at what she found, and come running back to him within the hour. But that had not happened, and he had set off to find Dirck Der Meer, only to meet with a second disappointment, and no indication as to where his friend might now be living.

At first he had toyed with the idea of

following after the girls, and calling at their new home, but he decided against it. Tomorrow he would hang around in St. Anthoiesbreestraat until Jacintha came to find him as she had promised. In the meantime he would set about finding some work, and at night he would bed down in the boat until the time came when he could afford to move into lodgings.

The shipyard was noisy with the sound of axe, saw, and hammer. Constantijn, walking along a wharf, kept slowing his pace to stare up at the great hulls in every stage of construction, his nostrils stinging from the smell of the compound of sulphur, tar and tallow with which some of them were being coated. Nearby the water was full of vessels, many under repair. An old 'wooden-wall' was ringed about with rafts holding a score of men, all at work, and others sat on narrow platforms suspended down the ship's sides.

Constantijn could have watched indefinitely, but firmly he turned away, and entered the first of the low, sprawling buildings to which he had been directed. The more comfortable and familiar aromas of wood and leather and glue greeted him. The carpenter in charge straightened up, put aside his saw, and regarded him intently with narrowed eyes.

'What do you want?' he demanded.

'Work,' Constantijn answered.

The carpenter set rough, work-scarred hands

on his hips, and questioned Constantijn as to experience, background, and apprenticeship. And Constantijn, who had prepared a fine story about working for his father in a country workshop, delivered his answer exactly how he had rehearsed it to himself on the boat. He was unaware that not a word he uttered was being believed.

Another runaway apprentice. The carpenter could spot them instantly with their rough country clothes, their soft dialects from Friesland, Gelderland, or South Holland, and their trumped-up excuses for being in Amsterdam; moreover their open eagerness for work showed their total ignorance of the shipyards' ever increasing and almost desperate need of all skilled and semi-skilled labour. At a time when Amsterdam was fast becoming the most flourishing trade centre in the world, and Dutch shipwrights were designing and building warships for many nations, it was not the time to question too closely about a man's credentials.

'You can start right away,' the carpenter said after making some show of deliberation. 'Let's see something of your ability before it gets dark.' Then a snap of his fingers brought one of his own apprentices forward at a run, and Constantijn was taken off through a shed stacked with floors, futtocks, and top-timbers to be set to the laborious and arduous task of smoothing off the great deck planks.

Constantijn, dusty, dirty, and utterly content, joined the stream of workmen going out from the shipyard some while later, and made his way into a nearby inn to buy himself a meal with some ale to quench his thirst. The work was not what he wanted, but it would give him a living until he had carved some pieces to present as examples of his art and craftsmanship to a master carver, and under the circumstances it was as well to approach by way of a carpenter's trade. He had his own gouges and chisels, which was fortunate, and the wharf was littered with stacks of wood, cast out blocks and lengths, which were used as fuel under the tar-cauldrons, and he had made up his mind to rescue any such piece that he felt he could put to good use. He had already pocketed a small block of finely-grained pear wood, which cut superbly and would be unsurpassed for the delicate piece of carving that he had in mind.

When he had finished eating he had a second tankard of ale, and sat back, watching the other people there. As the inn was close to one of the many landing stages where foreign ships were moored there was a buzz of alien tongues that mingled with local voices and dialects from other districts farther afield. There were plenty of seamen snatching time ashore, bent on a night of drinking and wenching, and at a corner table there was a quieter bunch from an English vessel, whose eyes travelled speculatively about the gathering as if some grim purpose lay behind their apparently casual survey.

Constantijn felt their gaze fall on him more than once, but each time he looked in their direction they had turned away again. He knew the ship they were from, having overheard the conversation between two shipyard workers sitting by him at the same table. It was a three-masted merchantman that had been caught in a squall off the coast, and ten men had been swept overboard by a freak wave that had caught them unawares. Constantijn concluded that the subdued humour of the Englishmen must be due to grief over the loss of their shipmates, which must surely explain their modest drinking and quiet conversation.

At last Constantijn rose, made his way between the crowded tables to the door, and went out into the night. The wind, blowing from the sea, smelt fresh and salty, stinging his nostrils pleasantly. He turned in the direction of the canal where he had left the boat, and was looking forward to some rest and a good night's sleep. His heart was light as he ambled along, whistling softly, and his thoughts were tenderly concerned with Jacintha. He did not hear the men that followed him silently in the shadows.

Then, just as he was about to pass from the narrow street into a square, a foot scraped on a stone just behind him. He spun about, more surprised than alarmed, and looked into a ring of set and ruthless faces. He recognized them instantly as the English seamen from the inn. A second later every one of them splintered into a thousand arrows of pain that plunged him down, down, down into a whirling pool of darkness.

CHAPTER FOUR

It seemed to Jacintha to be a night without end. She and Lysbeth lay huddled together under the tower walls, having chosen a spot within sight of the stone steps where the boat had been moored in the faint hope that Constantijn might return there with it. The stars began to fade at last as day brought the sun, making a gauzy mist over the canals, and filling the city with the sound of church bells. With some impatience Jacintha roused Lysbeth, who had slept without stirring the long hours through.

'I'm so hungry,' Lysbeth complained sulkily, rubbing the sleep from her eyes, her dark hair tumbling about her face.

'Get up,' Jacintha ordered briskly, already on her feet, and brushing the creases from her skirts. 'Today we must find Uncle Jurriaen, but I'll not ask you to start searching on an empty stomach. We'll spend one of the coins that

Constantijn paid me for the boat-hook.'

A baker's horn caught their attention as they started off, and a little way along the nearby street they found him with a basket of rusks on one arm, and loaves of new bread on the other. They devoured a loaf between them, and then set off for the Town Hall, which they located in the 'Dam', a wide square where already the fish market was doing a brisk trade.

The entrance hall of the ancient grey stone building was dank and cold, and full of merchants, gentlemen in fine clothes, and here and there an officer of the Civic Guard, all of whom seemed to be shown through the great oaken doors into the depths of the building without too much waiting, but others, humbler folk like themselves, were passed over time and time again by the grim-faced clerk, who sat at a high desk with a quill tucked behind his ear, and seemed to be expert at sorting the sheep from the goats. But eventually he beckoned the sisters forward, and listened not too impatiently to their request.

'The Haaring family lived on St. Catharinastraat for many years, you say? Well I'll see if anyone can help you.'

Another hour went by before he called them forward again, and they in turn were directed into one of the inner offices. There a rheumaticky old scribe, with full disorderly hair like a lion's mane, informed them that he was sure he remembered hearing that Mynheer Haaring was moving either to the Nez or the Niezel.

'You see, Juffrouw, compensation for the pulling down of those fine houses was paid long since,' he explained, tapping his forehead to indicate the strain on his memory, 'but I happened to be present when Mynheer Haaring called to complain about the figure first offered, which he declared insufficient to meet the cost of another residence that he intended to purchase. I seem to recall that one or other of those streets was mentioned in the discourse.'

It was little enough to help them on their way, but Jacintha was thankful to know for certain that Uncle Jurriaen was still in Amsterdam, and she and Lysbeth set off once again, determined to knock on every door in their narrowed search. But it proved to be a disappointing and often an humiliating experience when they were turned away frequently with more suspicion and hostility than with courtesy. None on the Niezel knew the name of Jurriaen Haaring.

It was early evening when they came to the Nez. There the houses were all tall and step-gabled, with fronts half-timbered, upper stories overhanging, and the sandstone and brickwork mellowed pleasantly to ochre and rose. An air of comfortable prosperity lay over the street.

'Let's hope we find Uncle Jurriaen here,' Jacintha said stoutly, buoying up her sister's flagging spirits. Lysbeth had become increasingly disheartened, and had given way to tears more than once, being tired, hungry again, and more than a little frightened.

Jacintha had become so used to the shaking of a head in answer to her enquiry that she stared in incredulous delight when a nod and a smile was finally given by a kindly-faced housewife.

'He lives in the fifth house on the far side,' she told Jacintha, and gently closed the door.

Jacintha spun about, and embraced Lysbeth. 'We've found him!' she cried, and then set off almost at a run, holding her sister by the hand. From here she could set out to search for Constantijn, unhampered by concern for Lysbeth, and surely she must find him, just as her diligence had been rewarded today. Her heart seemed to be crying out to him. And surely he must hear it?

'Tell Mynheer Jurriaen Haaring that his nieces, Jacintha and Lysbeth are here,' Jacintha announced jubilantly, and somewhat breathlessly, to the manservant that opened the door.

'My master has company, and may be engaged for some time,' he answered, unable to hide his surprise, his curious eyes taking in their humble clothes and country appearance.

'Then we'll wait,' Jacintha stated firmly, stepping inside, and ushering Lysbeth with her. The man looked dubious, but after a second's hesitation he showed them into an ante-room where the floor, as in the hall, was paved with black and white tiles, and walls covered with a splendid panelling, richly carved. He closed the door, and left them alone.

Jacintha sat down thankfully in a chair, but Lysbeth went darting about on a tour of inspection, all tiredness forgotten as she handled the silver vessels that stood on a side-table, peeped into a tall and beautiful cupboard, which contained a great number of books, and stood on tiptoe to trace the ship routes of the East India Company marked out on a hanging chart. Finally she fingered a curtain of yellow silk brocade that hung the length of one wall, more for dramatic effect than for any useful purpose, and then swept it against her, causing it to fall in heavy folds over one small, out-thrust foot.

'Look! Would this not make a magnificent gown?' she declared, and set the rings a-rattle on the rods, as she twisted and pranced about.

'Be still,' Jacintha implored wearily, but was ignored. It was some time before Lysbeth's interest in her surroundings began to wane, and she sat down sighing, and tapped her foot impatiently. It had become quite dark, but no candles had been brought, and there was a certain eeriness in being in that unfamiliar room in that silent house.

'Perhaps Uncle Jurriaen hasn't been told that we're here,' Lysbeth snapped, irritated by the anti-climax of it all.

'That's not likely,' Jacintha said calmly. 'Be patient. You do not know what important matters he might have in hand.'

Lysbeth scowled, refusing to be placated. 'Our home was poor enough, but no stranger ever set foot in it without some refreshment being offered. Why doesn't one of his family come forward to see that we are served wine, or some comforts?'

'He could be a bachelor.'

'I hadn't thought of that,' Lysbeth remarked with lifted eyebrows.

Then suddenly the door opened, and the manservant, holding high a candle, bade them follow him, making no apologies for lack of attention. Down a long passage they went, the sisters hand in hand, unaware that they clasped each other with the same intensity as in childhood when they had been frightened in dark woods, or alarmed by moon-shadows in the lane.

The salon they were shown into burst upon them with a blaze of light. The two girls, dazzled by the brilliance of so many candles after the gloom, paused blinking in the open doorway. Two middle-aged men stood talking by a table covered with a Turkish carpet, on which rested some documents, and a silver inkstand with some pens. But now they turned, their conversation dying away. The younger of them drew back slightly, but the elder, a grey-haired man in a black velvet gown with a white collar, glanced over his spectacles at the girls. His face was pigmented and wrinkled, the eyes shrewd, the lips tight, and he rested the knuckles of his hands on the table, arms straight, as he watched them approach.

Jacintha, slightly unnerved by the silence, the lack of any word of greeting, kept a firm grip on Lysbeth's trembling hand, and managed to speak out clearly. 'You must be our Uncle Jurriaen, sir.'

He acknowledged the curtsey that she gave him with a slight bow, but shook his head at her words. 'That is not so, Juffrouw.'

She glanced quickly towards the other man, whose ill-proportioned features were given a certain amount of charm by a wide, energetic mouth, his eyes bright and lively under bushy brows. 'I am not he, Juffrouw,' he said with a smile. 'My name is Pieter Pieterzoon.'

Jacintha looked bewildered. 'Then whom—?'

'Come here, Jacintha.' A beringed finger was beckoning to her from a large, high-backed chair drawn near to the chimney-piece. And Jacintha, startled, saw that she was being watched in a looking-glass hanging on the wall.

67

She looked back steadily at the reflection as she obeyed the summons. There, sitting back with long legs crossed, was an extravagantly dressed young man, his jacket and breeches of pale chamois leather, his short cloak of brown velvet tossed back with a silken gleam of greenish-bronze lining, and his shoulder-belt a-glitter with gold. His hollow-cheeked, Pan-like face was fair-skinned, his fronded hair and chin-tuft moustache ash-blond, and under limp lids his cold grey eyes were regarding her with a sly and curious interest. As she came round to stand facing him she saw that although not drunk he had had more than enough, and in his other hand an empty goblet dangled over the side of the chair.

'It seems I have made a mistake, and brought my sister to the wrong house,' she said, feeling faint with disappointment, and wondering how she could have been so foolish as to have assumed that there could be only one Jurriaen Haaring. It was not an uncommon name, and there would be many so called in such a large city as Amsterdam.

'On the contrary,' he remarked laconically, setting the goblet on a small side-table as he rose to his feet. He was very tall, lithe and lean, and the thickness of the wide and fashionable sash that he wore gave no illusion of weight to his slender body. He looked what he was: an egotist and a dandy; highly sensuous, with a streak of indolence in his nature controlled by a compelling ruthlessness that caused him always to seek the easiest way around any difficult matter that threatened his will or his comfort, even if it meant the momentary effort of crushing down anyone who stood in his path. Jacintha, who had not been reassured in any way, disliking his slightly caustic tone, was filled with apprehension when his next words confirmed that she had indeed come to the right house.

'I'm Jurriaen Haaring—the only son of the man that you expected to find here. Welcome to the bosom of the family, Cousins Jacintha—and Lysbeth.' He acknowledged the younger girl's presence with a dispassionate glance. 'Your father must be dead. You'd not be here for any other reason. The bottle was the cause of my father's demise, but the plague killed my mother years ago. What of yours?'

'The coughing sickness took her from us the winter before last,' Jacintha answered quietly, trying to overcome the instinctive aversion that she felt towards this new-found cousin.

'My condolences,' he said without expression, and turned slightly to bring the elderly man within the circle of their conversation. 'Now—allow me to present my friend and lawyer, Dr. Lödewÿck Doomer. It was his delay in getting here that caused you such a long wait in the ante-room. I apologize for that, but I didn't dare to receive you until he was here.' Then, ignoring Jacintha's puzzled frown, he clapped a hand on the shoulder of Pieter Pieterzoon. 'This fellow has already introduced himself. He's a shipwright, like myself, and was taking wine with me while we discussed the reckonings of a new vessel soon to be built. He has agreed to stay and act as witness to this business between we cousins that has to be settled.'

Jacintha's face tightened, and she lifted her chin slightly as she spoke. 'I cannot imagine what business that could be, Jurriaen. My sister and I have not come begging, and we want nothing from you. We came only to seek out your father, whom we had reason to believe would offer us a home under our grandfather's roof. But that house has gone, your father dead, and my promise to a dying man has been fulfilled, putting the matter to an end. Come, Lysbeth.' She put out her hand again to her sister. 'We're leaving at once.'

'Not so fast!' Jurriaen blocked her way, and an odd look of mingled alarm and cunning flickered in his eyes. 'We're an ill-fated family, Jacintha. None of us survives to any great age, and I'm impatient to get my hands on my share of our grandfather's guilders—not that he left any vast fortune! Far from it! But just hear what Dr. Doomer has to tell you first, I beg you!'

70

Jacintha, uncertain, fearful, half-turned towards the lawyer, but it was Pieter Pieterzoon who gave her a smile, and pushed forward a chair for her, and she felt that here was someone she could really trust. She sat down, her back very straight, resting her elbows on the arms, and Lysbeth settled quickly on a stool by her feet.

'Let me read you the terms of your grandfather's will, Juffrouw,' the lawyer said in his dry voice, taking up a document from the table. 'Then you may leave with all haste if you so wish, never to return, or remain in his household under the conditions laid down.'

Then he read the document aloud. It soon became clear both to Jacintha and Lysbeth that their mother had married Adriaen den Hartogh against Grandfather Haaring's wishes, running away with him, and bringing—in the eyes of the old man—disgrace upon the family. As time went on Grandfather Haaring, disappointed by the increasing dissipations of his only son, and prevented by pride from communicating with his daughter, changed his will in a mood of bitterness, and left everything to his grandson, Jurriaen, subject to strange and complicated conditions. As Jacintha listened to them her astonishment grew, and when the lawyer came to the end of the bequest a little silence fell. Then she spoke.

'I understand from what I have just heard

71

that my grandfather saw fit to prevent my cousin Jurriaen from inheriting the estate until he reaches his fortieth natal day.'

'Forty!' Jurriaen expostulated with a disgusted groan, and flung himself down into a chair, letting his booted feet thud on the floor.

'But,' Jacintha continued, 'this was only to ensure that my mother, if widowed, still had the chance to return like a prodigal daughter to her old home, in which case everything would have been hers, and Jurriaen left with the small annual sum that he draws now. But, as this was a highly unlikely possibility—my mother being a proud woman—a proviso was made that in the event of some act of God that resulted in any of her children becoming encumbrant upon Jurriaen as head of the family, then certain restrictions were to be withdrawn.'

The lawyer nodded. 'You have only to ask Jurriaen quite formally here before myself and this other witness for his legal protection to secure a home for yourself and your sister until such time as you may wish to marry, or until the end of your days. At the same time you will release the flow of a handsome income for Jurriaen which he so greatly desires.'

They were all watching her. Jurriaen, leaning forward, his knuckles white as he gripped the arms of his chair, his eyes angry with impatience. Pieter Pieterzoon's expression was one of unease, as though it troubled him to be present, but the lawyer's face was quite immobile as he waited for her to consider what he had said.

'If I make this request, Dr. Doomer,' Jacintha said carefully, 'does it mean that Lysbeth and I must become obedient to Jurriaen at all times of decision?'

'That is correct.' He nodded his head. 'Jurriaen becomes your legal guardian. Naturally you and your sister will have your own allowances paid from the estate, but he will control all other matters that may arise. I have a document drawn up here for you to sign.'

'Come, Jacintha!' Jurriaen exclaimed in exasperation. 'Take the pen!'

Still she hesitated. Her father had wanted her to seek a home for herself and Lysbeth with his brother-in-law, of whom her mother must have been fond, for all his faults, but would he have wished her to put their future into the hands of this young, headstrong man with his restless eyes and greedy mouth. She sensed cruelty at the core of him, and some indefinable quirk of slyness in his nature that made every sense within her contract and rear up in protest at the thought of becoming subject to him. Better to be free and make their own way as best they may.

'I cannot agree to it,' she pronounced quietly.

There was pandemonium. Jurriaen leapt to his feet, shouting at her, but it was Lysbeth who had shrieked out a wail of protest, hurling herself about to catch Jacintha by the wrists, jerking her forward in the chair.

'Don't deny me this chance!' Lysbeth cried in frantic appeal, panic crescent in her voice. 'This is what I've always wanted! A fine home! Comfort! Money to spend! All the clothes I could wish for!'

Jacintha took her wild, unhappy face between her hands. 'Trust me, Lysbeth. You'll not regret it in the end, I promise you. We'll manage well enough.'

'No!' Lysbeth struck away Jacintha's hands, and sprang up. 'I want to stay!'

'Well spoken, Lysbeth!' Jurriaen encouraged exuberantly, seeing now where his victory would lie.

'I've had my share of poverty and debtors and even of being hungry!' Lysbeth cried, at bay before her sister, fists clenched, and feet apart. 'I'm not willing to grovel for a living, even if you are! Have you forgotten why we came here? Because Papa wished it! You gave him your word!'

Jacintha rose, and faced the lawyer. 'I'd like to discuss this in private with my sister.'

'No! No!' Lysbeth shrieked, stamping her foot. 'There's nothing that you could say in a thousand years that would take me from this place, Jacintha! Leave if you wish! I'll not try to stop you—but I'm staying!'

74

There was a taut, strained moment of silence. And Jacintha saw such a dark look of contained triumph on Jurriaen's face that she felt her heart tighten with fear. She realized that she must act instantly to prevent Lysbeth being coerced into putting her solitary signature to the document of agreement, which would remove her beyond all bounds of outside help.

'I have a suggestion to make,' Jacintha said with an air of confidence that hid the unhappy whirlpool of her emotions. 'As you know, my father assigned Lysbeth's well-being to my charge, and I'm wholly responsible for her. Let me retain some voice in her future, and I'll put my name to that paper.'

'What had you in mind?' Dr. Doomer enquired, leaning forward slightly as though to protect with his shadow across the document his client's interests.

'When I marry that Lysbeth shall have equal freedom to absolve herself from Jurriaen's guardianship if she so desires, and make her home with me. From that time forward his authority is at an end.'

Dr. Doomer looked at Jurriaen over his spectacles. 'What do you say? It's a reasonable request, and an admirable solution to this little impasse.'

Jurriaen smiled, but his eyes were deadly. 'I have no objection. Let it be that way.'

Jacintha saw that he would never forgive her

for this first meeting when she had nearly sabotaged his chance of an early inheritance, made him feel slightly foolish before the two other men, and finally brought him to her own terms. Altogether he was a man to be reckoned with, and she knew she had made an enemy. But Lysbeth's joy and relief were exultant, and Jacintha realized how close she had come to alienating herself from the very one that she had sworn to protect. But her heart was heavy and full of doubt as she submitted to her sister's thankful embrace, and her hand shook as she took the quill and signed the document.

Supper was served afterwards, and Jurriaen, although he drank heavily, declaring it to be an occasion for celebration, behaved impeccably. After the other two men had left he rang for the maidservant to show them up to the adjacent bed-chambers that had been prepared for them. Lysbeth bade him goodnight with an impulsive kiss on the cheek, which made him glance at her in amused surprise, and then darted off after the maid and the dancing candle, eager to see her new quarters. But Jurriaen checked Jacintha when she would have followed.

'I'll expect you to take charge of the keys tomorrow, and run this house efficiently for our mutual comfort and convenience. The servants take advantage of a bachelor, you know. They're a lazy, ignorant trio in the kitchen, and I suspect that the accounts I have to settle for food and wine are far in excess of what should be paid. Dismiss them if you wish, and start afresh.'

'I'll look into the matter,' she answered, glad that he had made this request to housekeep of her. It would be a pleasure to take care of this fine house. 'Good night, Jurriaen.'

He did not answer, but followed her across the hall, and stood at the foot of the staircase to watch her as she went up, the candle she held capturing her face in its pale flickering light.

'Oh, Jacintha,' he remarked carelessly, causing her to pause and look down at him. 'There's something I'd like to ask you.'

'What is that?' A pang of apprehension went fluttering through her.

'That little clause you insisted upon interested me very much.' He set his hand upon the carved newel post, his rings catching the candlelight. 'About my guardianship of Lysbeth coming to an end automatically upon the occasion of your marriage. Tell me—have you anyone in mind to take to husband?'

She guarded her answer. 'I have no immediate plans.'

He smiled slowly and cruelly. 'I'm so glad to hear that. You see, Jacintha, you overlooked one small point. You'll have to get my permission to wed in the first place. And that, I warn you, will depend entirely upon my carefully considered opinion of the suitor in question. It could be that Lysbeth becomes a bride long before I see fit to release you from spinsterhood.'

Then he turned about, and went back into the salon, closing the door behind him. Jacintha stayed where she was, staring after him, stunned by the threat of his words. Then slowly she continued up the staircase, filled with dread at what might lie ahead in a future from which all personal freedom had been signed away. It seemed as though the bars of a cage had snapped shut about her.

She could not sleep. The four-poster bed was more comfortable than the narrow cupboard bed at home, its pillows soft, its linen finely woven, but although her whole body ached with weariness her mind was alert and active, churning over the strange situation in which she and Lysbeth had found themselves, and wondering how long it would be before she and Constantijn found each other again. Suppose months passed while they searched blindly for each other in this teeming city without ever making contact?

The thought filled her with such panic that she threw back the bed-covers, and went across to lean her forehead against the cool glass of the latticed window. Amsterdam, set amid its forests of tall masts, spread out on all sides, a-twinkle with lights.

'Where are you, Constantijn?' Jacintha

whispered in despair. 'Oh find me soon, sweet love!'

Constantijn was lying sleepless too, his arm under his head, in a dark corner of the lower deck that rose and fell with the ploughing of the ship through the waves. He had not wept or cursed or gone almost berserk as had the other unfortunates pressed against their will into service on the English vessel, but on shaking his aching head in consciousness of what had befallen him, he had reeled to his feet and rushed to hurl himself over the bulwarks, intent on swimming for shore while Amsterdam still lay upon the horizon. But he was not the first to try that trick, and he had had been brought crashing down by a couple of burly seamen posted for just such an occurrence.

Thinking it over he realized that in a way they had saved his life, for in his dazed, still half-stunned state, he would most surely have drowned immediately, but the only thought in his head had been that he was being taken away from Jacintha. Where was she now? Lying asleep in her soft bed with her silken hair tumbled on the pillow, her long lashes flickering as she stirred in quiet dreams, as she had done that night on the little boat when he had held her in his arms. Or was she awake? Some sixth sense telling her that all was not well? He wondered if today she had been to find him at Dirck der Meer's old rooms in St.

Anthoiesbreestraat as she had promised, and discovered that he was not there. What would she think when no word came from him? It was only too easy to surmise that. She would wait and wait until gradually doubt set in, and then she would come to believe that his promises and words of love had been nothing more than a brief summer incident between passing strangers.

The thought caused him such distress that he rolled over and buried his face in his arm, his body taut and twisted. It was impossible to keep back the fear that he would never see her again, and his desolation was absolute.

★   ★   ★

Every day Jacintha went out looking for Constantijn. The boat was never at the moorings where they had intended it to be left, and another visit to the Town Hall gave her the information that nobody else had enquired after the new address of Mynheer Haaring. As time went on she became increasingly anxious, every knock on the door sending her rushing to open it, and she herself took in any letter delivered in the faint hope that he might have located her after all.

'We have those new servants you've employed to perform these duties,' Jurriaen remarked.

Only to Lysbeth did he pay any attention, quick to praise with lavish compliments the new clothes that she bought with abandon, squandering her allowance as soon as it was received. It amused him to see her blush hotly while noticing out of the corner of his eye how Jacintha grew tense and prickly as a watchdog. But at other times Lysbeth's ingenuousness bored him, and he treated her with complete indifference. Then she withdrew, hurt and quiet, and would speak to no one, certain that somehow Jacintha was to blame, for she resented bitterly her sister's reserved attitude towards their guardian, knowing that it had its roots in misgivings and mistrust, while she herself could see no wrong in him.

Looking back, Jacintha was able to pin-point the beginning of her sister's infatuation to the moment when Jurriaen had risen from his chair on that evening they had arrived at the house in the Nez. Lysbeth, so young, inexperienced, and highly impressionable, had been wholly dazzled by Jurriaen's deceptively wistful good looks, and then her adoration had been given strength by the conviction that he alone was responsible for delivering her from all the miseries that had beset both her and Jacintha, and which would have claimed them again if he had not been willing to take them in. His motive was of no importance to her.

Yet on the whole the sisters saw little of

Jurriaen. He went out on his own affairs most evenings, and often did not return all night. He spent the greater part of each day in his office at the shipyard, and invariably came home in the company of other shipwrights like himself when the talk was always of gunwales and galleries, draught, decks, and displacements, and there hung about the cloaks left in the hall a peculiar salty aroma of sea-timbers, tar, new rope, and tallow.

Sometimes Pieter Pieterzoon was in the company, and he always had a word and a smile for the girls. It was he who saw that they were lonely and neglected socially in what was essentially a bachelor's stronghold, and as a result Jacintha and Lysbeth found themselves invited to the Pieterzoon's home. Pieter, who was a notable shipwright, senior both in age and experience to Jurriaen and the others, frequently entertained representatives of foreign governments, merchants, and company owners, and the sisters were often called upon to use their French in discourse with these gentlemen.

They had clothes for all occasions, and included among the garments in Jacintha's well-stocked closet was a warm crimson cloak that she used for her daily walk. She had come to know every corner of Amsterdam from the Rugulierspoort to the Damrak, and could name every building of importance from the Exchange to the weighing-house. Many times she thought she saw Constantijn in the crowded fish market, or strolling by the houses of the Bierkade or the Oude Zijds Voorburgwal, or even passing by in a barge, or on a sailing-vessel. But always there was disappointment as an unfamiliar profile was turned towards her, and more than once she had stood half-blinded with tears, careless of those who stared at her distress.

Only to Pieter Pieterzoon, that reliable, kindly man, did she finally confess that she was trying to find someone of importance to her. She sought him out at his own home, and there he and his wife, Saartje, a rosy, healthy-looking woman, who wore her soft copper-coloured hair in bunches of curls that hung like grapes over her ears, listened to her appeal.

'What an unhappy trick of fate to separate you from this young Constantijn on the very day of your arrival in Amsterdam!' Saartje exclaimed, her round face full of compassion.

'How may I help you?' Pieter asked courteously.

'I want to visit all the places in the yards where wood-carvers are to be found at work. Could you arrange this for me?'

Neither Pieter nor his wife thought to suggest that this request might as well have been put to Jurriaen, for the very fact that Jacintha had turned for outside help told them that there must be little liking for each other between the

83

two cousins.

'That's quite an order.' Pieter commented with a smile, 'but I have just the one to escort you—my nephew, Symon, who is in the supplies office. He knows every studio and work-shop in Amsterdam.'

Thus it was that Lysbeth, who accompanied Jacintha on the round of work-shops, which proved to be a fruitless search, met Symon Pieterzoon for the first time. He was fair-bearded and personable, and was much taken with her from the moment of meeting, but it was too late. Lysbeth had become infatuated with Jurriaen, and the constant worry of this new matter hung over Jacintha like an additional cloud.

CHAPTER FIVE

'Jacintha! Where are you?' Lysbeth's urgent voice went ringing through the house.

In the salon Jacintha dropped her embroidery, and hurried to open the door. 'Here! What is it?'

Lysbeth, snowflakes lying like a veil over her fur hood, her face flushed by both the bitter weather outside and an inner excitement, threw aside muff and mittens as she entered, and clasped her sister by the arms.

'I've just come from the shipyard! Jurriaen took me to see the Spanish galleon under repair there—and while we were in the office I heard some news of interest to you!'

'Constantijn?' Jacintha cried on a wild surge of hope.

Lysbeth shook her head. 'No! But Dirck der Meer! Remember? The friend that Constantijn was going to stay with in St. Anthoiesbreestraat!'

'What did you hear? Tell me!'

Lysbeth, breathless, unfastened her cloak as she talked. 'A clerk in the next office was reading aloud a list that was being checked off—carpenters, smiths, cabinet-makers, and a lot of other workmen who had completed work on a warship for the French navy, and were to be paid off today before they dispersed to yards in Rotterdam, and other parts. Then suddenly I caught der Meer's name.' She giggled. 'I just burst through the half-open door, and ordered the clerk to repeat the name—which he did!'

'Paid off today!' Jacintha exclaimed. 'I must see him—there's just a chance that he has met with Constantijn somewhere!'

'That's what I thought. I've written down the name of the ship, and the berth where it lies.' She pulled a piece of paper from her pocket, and laughed as Jacintha snatched it from her. 'You'll have to hurry. They'll be leaving the yard at any time this afternoon!'

85

'I'll take the sledge! Get it ready for me!' Jacintha went running up the stairs to throw open the closet doors, and there came a sweet fragrance from the pomanders that hung amongst her clothes as she snatched out her cloak, and kicked off her yellow shoes to thrust her feet into soft leather boots. Then down she went again, and found that one of the menservants was waiting at the door with the high-backed, shell-shaped sledge. Lysbeth, ready with a fur wrap, tucked it about Jacintha's knees as soon as she had settled herself on its single seat.

'Good fortune go with you!' Lysbeth said warmly, and for a few moments the two sisters recaptured that easy relationship that had always been between them until the dark figure of Jurriaen had loomed up in their lives.

'Thank you, Lysbeth,' Jacintha said gratefully. Then the sledge was off, the manservant running with it, along the Nez. Not until he had guided it down a snow slope on to the ice did he release it and step back on to the bank again. Jacintha set the two iron-shod steering-stocks into their sockets, and with a quick thrust the shell-shaped sledge shot away, its scarlet paintwork gleaming in the blue-white afternoon, the light snow swirling about her.

Past the ice-locked barges and boats she flew, across one canal and into another, and under bridges hung with icicles where the hiss of runners echoed as loudly as the roar of a waterfall. Skaters darted from her path, and other sledges, proceeding at a more leisurely rate, steered to one side to let her go skimming through. Some youths, playing golf upon the ice, waved their sticks and cheered as she flashed by, but at the speed she was travelling she did not dare to wave back, but kept her attention on the way ahead, and her hands ready to change her direction at a moment's notice.

But suddenly, as the canal curved, and a jutting quay hid her immediate view, a large carved and gilded sledge, its prow dragon-headed, shot into sight, bearing a driver and two passengers, and came swooping down on her.

'Look out!' she screamed, and half rose from her seat to thrust with her right stick. The dragon-head swept crimson and gilt past her face as the sledges escaped collision with only inches to spare. But she was too hard upon the bank to escape disaster, and although she plunged with the other stick, scoring the ice into glittering crystals, her little shell-sledge was out of control. It spun wildly, and with a great shudder crashed against the snow-covered bank. A runner snapped with a sound loud as a musket-shot amid a splintering of wood, and Jacintha was tossed out, and sent spinning across the ice amid fur-wrap and whirling sticks and smashed sledge. Then she lay still and crumpled, her eyes closed, and her face as pale as the white wintry sky above.

At first the thundering in her head was too great to be borne. And the waves of oblivion that came and went gave only brief but blissful moments of respite. Only when Jacintha felt herself being lifted up did she manage to raise lids heavy with pain, and her blurred gaze became focused on the face of the man in whose arms she lay. A stranger. Eyes very blue. Like the Zuider Zee in summertime. Too bright, too piercing to meet without some softening shade.

'Who are you? What is your name?' His voice was very deep, and he spoke Dutch with an accent that was entirely unfamiliar to her. She tried to answer him, but the drumming in her head was so loud that she knew it would drown her whisper, and in any case the effort involved was defeating her. She concentrated on his mouth. It was a well-cut, love-weathered mouth. Forming words that seemed to reach her consciousness aeons after they had been spoken. Addressing those who had come rushing to the scene. 'Is there no one here who recognizes this lady?'

Their encircling faces swam about her, mingling with the snow-covered roofs of the gabled houses that rose high against the sky on each side of the canal, but although there was murmuring from those gathered there none answered up. And then once more everything whirled into darkness.

A candle flame glowed like a small sun. She watched it through her lashes. The feather quilt that covered her in its warmth was encouraging her lethargy. What was the time? Would the maid soon come to wake her? Why had she forgotten to snuff out the candle before retiring? Retiring? Vividly there sprang to mind the whole calamitous incident on the ice. She had lost her chance of speaking with Dirck der Meer! It was already night, and he would have gone on his way long since!

She sat up quickly, but a shaft of pain pierced her head, and she sank back again against the lace-edged pillows. She was not in her own bed! Nor in her own nightshift! This bedchamber with its painted murals on the walls was entirely unfamiliar to her! Where was she? And who had brought her here? The man that had gathered her up from the ice?

She rolled her head round to look towards the windows. No clue from any view there. Already the night frost had made silver lace over the panes, veiling the outside world from her. It gave her a strange sensation of being suspended in space and time. As though in some way the crash on the ice had ended the past, and she was being held in limbo until the moment came to set her upon a new, unknown way that she must follow.

But she must find out where she was. Again she made herself sit up, but she moved very carefully this time as she would have done had a book been balanced on her head. The painful throbbing did not lessen, but at least there were no blinding arrows to pin her down again. She dragged aside the quilt to put her feet to the floor. She was amazed at the weakness of her legs, and had to make her way with agonizing slowness towards the door, clutching first at the bedcurtains, and then at the solid arm of a chair.

She caught sight of her reflection in a looking-glass. How pale she looked! How dark about the eyes! She went closer to the glass, and peered in dismay at her appearance, seeing how shock still lingered in the dilation of her pupils, making the greyish-blue irises appear to be almost non-existent. Then she lifted one hand and trailed her fingertips over the inflamed bruises that disfigured her face.

At that moment the door opened, and to her wild relief it was Saartje Pieterzoon who paused on the threshold, her wide lace cap quivering as delicately as the wings of a night moth, and a look of alarm on her face at the sight of Jacintha out of bed.

'Jacintha! You shouldn't be on your feet!'

'I know that now,' Jacintha said, swaying forward, and Saartje caught her as her legs gave way.

It was wonderfully pleasant to be hustled back into bed, tucked up, and fussed over. Moreover the relief at finding herself to be in the Pieterzoon's house was overwhelming, and completely dispelled that almost eerie feeling that she had experienced while not knowing exactly where she was. There were so many questions that she wanted to ask, but Saartje would have none of them until the last crease in the pillows had been smoothed, and Jacintha had swallowed a draught that the physician had left for her to take upon recovering consciousness.

'To think that you should have stirred in the few moments that you were left alone!' Saartje threw up her hands in self-reproach. 'You had a very bad fall on the ice. The sledge was smashed beyond repair, and we're lucky not to have you in a similar state. We informed Jurriaen, and he and Lysbeth came at once with the sleigh to take you home, but the physician will not have you moved from this bed until he sees fit. Lysbeth was sitting at your bedside until I called her down to sup with us.'

'But why was I brought under your roof in the first place, Saartje?' Jacintha persisted, and would have raised herself up from the pillows if Saartje had not pressed her gently down again. 'The last thing I remember is being held in the arms of one of the passengers in the sledge that almost collided with mine.'

91

A little smile played about Saartje's lips as she seated herself in a chair drawn up by the bed. 'Oh, you were conscious then? He thought not, for although your lids flickered open your eyes were glazed, and their sense seemed shut.'

'Who was that man?'

'Captain Axel Halvarsen—a Swedish government official. He had been in Amsterdam for a month on various matters, and was on his way to the ship that was taking him home again when the accident happened. He was afraid that you would die if you didn't receive immediate care, and saw to you himself instead of leaving it to others as most gentlemen as highly born as he would have done.'

'I heard him asking if anyone knew my name,' Jacintha said thoughtfully. So he was a Swede. No wonder his eyes were so blue. She tried to recall the rest of his features. His mouth was clear enough, but his face as a whole was vague and unformed, still viewed through the haze of pain created at the time. 'What made him bring me to your house?'

'He has been here to see Pieter on business several times, and knew this address to be near at hand. He could not delay long, and thought it best to leave you in our charge, knowing that we would set about finding out your identity, and locating those who would be most concerned for you. You can imagine his astonishment when we declared your name at once!' Then her inscrutable smile widened: 'He stayed as long as he could, and was much interested to hear all about you, but even then he had to leave before the physician came.'

A resentment, which she knew to be unreasonable and yet could not help, smouldered within Jacintha. It was entirely the fault of Axel Halvarsen that she had lost the golden chance to see Dirck der Meer that Lysbeth had put into her hands. That he had not been steering the sledge was of no consequence. She hoped that their paths would never cross again.

'Will he be coming back to The Netherlands?' she asked, succumbing to the drowsiness that the draught had brought upon her.

'I think not. His business here is finished.'

She closed her eyes with a feeling of thankfulness. It was amazing how much one could dislike a person about whom one knew so little.

*   *   *

Jacintha thought herself fortunate to have escaped any broken bones, but the physician kept her lying a-bed most of the day until the last of the minor headaches that plagued her as a result of the accident were quite gone. She was grateful for Saartje's care and attention through these many weeks, and for her friend's insistence upon Lysbeth staying in the house to be near her. Was it possible that Saartje shared her mistrust of Jurriaen, and had been determined not to leave the girl alone under the same roof with him?

During her days of convalescence Jacintha had plenty of time to think over all aspects of the affair, but for a long time it had lain like a gulf between the sisters, a subject to be avoided at all costs.

Seated near the fire in the Pieterzoons' entrance hall, Jacintha passed many of the long hours of enforced idleness in sketching. She did several studies of Lysbeth curled up on a window seat, whose thoughts were so obviously full of Jurriaen, hands idle in her rose silk lap, her abstracted gaze turned blindly towards a view of the sunlit houses on the opposite side of the canal where the lime trees were thrusting forth their buds.

'Let's go home soon,' Lysbeth said suddenly one day, glancing over her shoulder at Jacintha. 'I'm sure you're well enough, but you like it here. I'm tired of the Pieterzoons' company.'

Jacintha's stick of charcoal paused for a moment, and then continued shading in the dark folds of Lysbeth's glossy hair. 'The Pieterzoons? Or do you mean—just Symon?'

'He bores me with his attentions,' Lysbeth answered flatly. 'But I cannot forbid his coming

94

to this house.'

'We are an unfortunate pair, you and I,' Jacintha commented cautiously. 'Both of us loving in vain.'

'Don't say that!' Lysbeth had flung herself about, her dark eyes flashing mingled anger and distress. 'Just because your lover has proved false you distrust all men!'

Jacintha's colour drained away. 'That's not true. I know Constantijn still loves me!'

Lysbeth gave a derisive snort. 'If he did, he would have sought you out by now! But not he! He made off with our boat after filling your head with a pack of lies! How do we know that a word of what he told us was the truth? You're a fool, Jacintha! He was a cheat and a thief!'

Jacintha sprang up and flew at Lysbeth, the sketches fluttering away across the black and white tiled floor, and shook her furiously. Then she spun away, and brought her clasped and trembling hands up against her lips, ashamed at having given way to temper.

'You spit-cat,' Lysbeth remarked incredulously, easing her shoulder as if fearing there had been dislocation.

'I'm sorry I did that,' Jacintha apologized on a choke of distress, 'but I cannot allow you to speak like that of Constantijn.'

'Then let me have no more hints and innuendoes about Jurriaen! I mean to have him! No other man will do for me!' Lysbeth stated fiercely and irrevocably.

The next day they went back to the house in the Nez. They found most of the furniture covered with dust-sheets. Jurriaen looked up from sorting papers and documents in a walnut bureau.

'You'd better start packing. We're leaving for Stockholm next week. I've been offered the chance to work there under the Netherlands' greatest ship-builder—Hendrick Hybertsson himself.'

'I'll not go!' Jacintha declared vehemently.

He did not bother to glance again in her direction. 'You have no choice. I'm closing this house. You cannot stay on here.'

'You cannot make me leave my own country!'

Then he did turn towards her, his eyes darkly impatient, and spoke with sarcastic candour: 'As your legal guardian I must look after you and do what I think best for your well-being. You forget that those were the terms of our grandfather's will—and the estate pays me handsomely for that chore. How else could I settle my gaming debts?'

'I'll go back to the Pieterzoons! That could be arranged! Lysbeth and I can live with them!'

'Not I,' Lysbeth stated resolutely. 'I'd rather go to Sweden!'

Then Jacintha knew that as Jurriaen had said, there was no choice for her, for she could not let Lysbeth go alone. She flung the back of her hand across her mouth to keep back a sob, and went from the room. Their conversation followed her across the hall.

'What kind of ship will you be building, Jurriaen?'

'A man-o'-war for the Swedish navy—its reckonings drawn up by the Master himself.'

'What is it to be called?'

'The *Wasa*.'

CHAPTER SIX

Jurriaen would have found the voyage from Amsterdam to Stockholm excessively tedious if it had not been for Lysbeth. The sea was rough, keeping most of the other passengers in their berths, and when they did appear they proved to be poor company. Jacintha had remained at the taffrail gazing after Amsterdam with all the passionate distress of a prisoner being deported to the Indies, her cloak and skirts billowing, not moving until long after it had been lost from sight. Each day afterwards she had taken a solitary stroll up and down the deck when the weather and the roll of the ship permitted, paying him no attention.

But Lysbeth was a different matter. She had never been to sea before, and she was everywhere, a darting, laughing, exhilarated figure, her black hair streaming, arms out-flung as though to embrace the buffeting of the wind, and her white petticoats all a-tumble. She seemed intoxicated by the sea air, and he began to look at her with a new interest.

He had been appreciative of her dark beauty ever since she had begun to ripen peach-like before his eyes. The fashionable little velvet jackets with the tulip sweep of silken skirts in a contrasting colour suited both sisters admirably, but from the very first Lysbeth had worn hers with a kind of flamboyance, which—had he been so inclined—might have led to some small indiscretion on his part. But he had his own divertissements, and wanted neither the domestic upheaval that would result from a clash with the ever-protective Jacintha, who watched over her young sister like a lioness with a cub, nor the turbulent aftermath that invariably followed any affair with a woman in which he became involved.

He had long since realized vaguely that in some way the ambivalence of the relationship that he had had with his dominating mother, combined with the contempt he had felt for his amiable, weak-willed father, had somehow resulted in his never being able to feel deeply for any other human being. He had never experienced any sense of loss through it; on the contrary, he was wholly uninhibited in the gratification of his own selfish desires, and was only frustrated when circumstances contrived against him, forcing him to concede to the will of others. The invitation to Sweden had been like the opening of a door; he foresaw that after two or three years working in close association with such a renowned man as Hendrick Hybertsson, he would find every shipyard in the Netherlands clamouring for his services upon his return. Then wealth and power would be his, and there would be no more bowing down to lesser men.

Now for the first time it occurred to him that a beautiful and nubile young ward might prove to be an important asset during his time in Sweden. It was not in golden riksdaler that he considered her value, but in influential connections that might advance his fortunes while abroad. To Jacintha he did not give a thought, knowing that he could not manipulate her to suit his purpose, but Lysbeth, who made no secret of her devotion to him, ever gazing at him with entranced eyes, would be more than willing to do anything he asked of her. He decided to move in with smile, touch, and glance to cement this state of affairs, choosing an opportune moment when Lysbeth had clashed with Jacintha for refusing to go below when the sky had gathered for a storm, the rain already slashing down and pitting the turbulent sea.

'I like it!' Lysbeth shouted to him above the

noise of the wind and waves, holding her hood tight under her chin, her face wet with rain. 'It's exciting! Exhilarating! I want to watch the sea in all its moods on this voyage! Jacintha is afraid I'll get swept overboard. She fusses too much!'

'Of course she does,' he agreed, but drew her away from the rail and into shelter by a companionway. 'It's high time she realized that she must stop forever trying to interfere with your life. She'd have prevented you coming to Sweden with me if she'd had her way. Remember you're a grown woman now—and a very lovely one.'

Lysbeth raised her eyes to him. He was gazing at her with mingled amusement and severity as he stood propped by one shoulder against the wall, his coat collar turned up, and the rain dripping from the broad brim of his high crowned hat. The colour rose into her cheeks.

'It makes me happy that you see me so, Jurriaen.' Her voice was low, and he guessed rather than heard the words.

'Continue to be subject only to me, Lysbeth. Am I not your guardian? Is it not I alone whom you should seek to please?'

'Oh, that is my only wish!' she answered fervently. 'Always!'

'Then let's celebrate your vow by facing the elements!' He flung an arm about her shoulders, and together they went right up the forecastle, and held on as the bow split the choppy waves, and spray and rain and wind lashed into them until the Captain himself ordered them below.

It was a calm, bright day when they sailed into Swedish waters a week later. Jurriaen leaned on the gunwale, his eyes narrowed against the dazzling light, his gaze intent on the scenery. Lysbeth was at his side, flushed and happy, full of hope for the future. Only Jacintha stood apart, wondering how long it would be before she saw the canals and windmills of her own country once again.

The ship drew slowly in to the crowded quay at Dalarö, which was the main port of call for Stockholm, and there was such bustle and confusion when they stepped ashore that it was pleasant to have a way to a waiting coach cleared for them by a fellow countryman, thick-set and heavy-jowled, who introduced himself as Reyndert Leeghwater, representative of the Dutch Guild of Shipwrights. His own servants were left to see to the luggage, and convey it all the way to his residence in Stockholm when unloaded.

'It is customary for me to offer immediate hospitality to any new arrivals of importance from the homeland,' he explained with snobbish emphasis, his smile revealing teeth so sparsely set that it appeared at first that several

101

must be missing. But his mouth was exceptionally wide, thin-lipped and incisive, and his broad, square face seemed set about it, ruddy in hue, with a hooked nose, and eyes that were small, piercing, and intelligent, missing nothing that went on about him. In one swift absorbing glance he had taken in every detail of Jacintha's appearance, and noted the more abundant curves of the younger sister. It was with a stirring of anticipation that he handed them both into the coach, and stood aside for Jurriaen to enter. Then he gave a barked order to the coachman, and climbed in to take his seat beside Jurriaen, closing the door behind him.

'I'm glad to hear that we haven't to put up in some hostelry for the time being,' Jurriaen remarked as the wooden wheels began to roll forward over the cobbles.

'I must say that most people, unless they already have connections here, are very relieved to find me waiting for them.' One of his quick, side-long glances slipped over the girls, who were leaning together towards the right-hand window, exclaiming over the bright blue and yellow uniforms of a handful of soldiers marching along with helmets and breast-plates agleam in the sun. 'It gives a breathing space in which to find a suitable residence—not very easy with so many foreigners in the city. There's always money to be made in a country girding itself for new battles, although the

Swedish government is notoriously tight-fisted, and sometimes trouble blows up on all sides, especially when work has been contracted out, and subcontracted again, so that everybody is clamouring to be paid at the same time.'

'You paint a sorry picture of the state of affairs,' Jurriaen commented wryly. 'But there must be little doubt in peoples' minds that Gustavus Adolphus will ultimately transform his impoverished country into one of the great powers of Europe, or else nobody would stay. Rats are quick enough to leave a sinking ship.'

'True enough,' Reyndert conceded, but tapped Jurriaen's arm with a warning finger. 'Mark you, much could happen to influence the course of events. Sigismund of Poland, and the formidable Wallenstein, the Hapsburg Emperor's greatest general, will not rest until Gustavus Adolphus lies slain upon a battlefield.'

'But the Princess Christina is over a year old now, so he would leave an heir.'

Reyndert grimaced with meaning. 'If she survives. There have been attempts on her life already. A balcony collapsed on her cradle not long after she was born—it was no accident, that you can be certain of.' Then seeing that both girls had turned, startled, to listen to him, he gave his ugly smile in reassurance. 'Nothing happened to her that time.'

'Who would do such a thing?' Jacintha asked with horror.

Reyndert shrugged, his face bland. 'The King has many enemies.'

Although Stockholm proved to be as water-set as Amsterdam there was little resemblance between the flourishing trade centre which they had left behind, and this gaunt clustering of black-timbered buildings split apart by forest and lake and sea. The city was dominated by the Royal Castle of Three Crowns, which stood surrounded by massive castellated walls, its circular tower and copper-roofed turrets seeming to pierce the clear blue sky. It was the home of the warrior king, Gustavus Adolphus, and his German Queen, Maria Eleonora.

By contrast Reyndert Leeghwater's house had a mellow charm, and although local wood had been used, the Dutch architect had managed to capture the look of a Netherlands country house, and it was comfortably set in pleasant gardens. It had many rooms, and was large enough to have accommodated several families without their having to meet each other, but at the moment Jurriaen and the girls were the only guests. Every piece of furniture was Dutch, delicately ornamented with marquetry, and land- and seascapes covered the walls; even the plain plank floors, customary in Swedish homes, had been relaid with black and white tiles, and the floral designs on the ceilings obliterated with whitewash. Only the scenery beyond the latticed windows showed that it was not the residence of a Dutch burgher in the heart of Amsterdam. It was obvious that Reyndert Leeghwater was a Netherlander through and through, and wanted no truck with alien ways and customs; even the food, served that night at supper, included a familiar fish dish, and cheeses that had come with the ship.

When the meal was over Jacintha and Lysbeth retired, leaving the two men sitting on at the table.

'You're a fortunate fellow to have two such charming wards,' Reyndert commented, refilling his guest's glass with wine, and then his own. 'Young unmarried Dutch women are very scarce here—you'll have to keep an eye on them. There'll be plenty of suitors among the Dutch merchants that they'll meet. We Netherlanders prefer our own kind—the Swedish women are all fire and ice, but marriage with a foreigner is not to our taste.'

Jurriaen, well aware that Reyndert was putting out a feeler, regarded him under his languid lids with guarded amusement. Did the fool think that he hadn't noticed the marked attention towards Lysbeth throughout the meal? No doubt Jacintha's fair looks were too composed and quiet to be of interest to Mynheer Reyndert, but Lysbeth's almost voluptuous beauty had been well scrutinized out of the corner of those sliding eyes.

'Naturally I shall be pleased to consider any suitable candidates,' Jurriaen remarked evenly.

'Make certain that you select those who will show their gratitude,' Reyndert said with meaning, to all intents studying the colour of his wine.

'I'll most certainly heed your advice, sir.' Jurriaen inclined his head, and raised his glass to Reyndert, who responded with his own, and immediately their joint mood became more convivial. 'Now tell me about the *Wasa*,' Jurriaen continued, sitting back comfortably, 'and how far she has progressed. I know little beyond the fact that her keel was laid last year.'

'Yet I'm sure you're well aware of the reason for building her. A powerful fleet is indispensable to the King if he is to keep control of the Baltic, and the *Wasa* is the second of two large ships which—together with two smaller vessels—were ordered by him to strengthen his navy. Unfortunately the *Wasa* has been beset with difficulties all the way, and now with Hendrick Hybertsson lying at death's door—'

'What!' Jurriaen gave an involuntary start, and jerked his glass, making the wine slop over, and it trickled down the stem to drip upon his knee.

Reyndert raised his thin brows. 'Did you not know? But, of course, how could you! He was taken ill in the shipyard when you were about two days out from Amsterdam.'

'That's terrible news for me!' Jurriaen remarked bitterly, savage with disappointment, seeing the prestige and honour he had expected snatched away from him. 'Who is in charge now?'

'Hein Jacobsson, and Hendrick's brother, Arent.'

'God's teeth!' Jurriaen emptied his glass at a gulp, and thrust it forward to be filled again. 'I know Jacobsson. He's not an easy man to work with, and Arent Hybertsson de Groot is more merchant than shipwright.'

'You see no end to the *Wasa*'s troubles then?' Reyndert asked with interest, setting down the decanter, and he linked his thick fingers on the table before him.

Jurriaen lifted an impatiently placating hand. 'I've nothing to say against Jacobsson's ability, but I've no liking for the man. He made mock of a vessel of mine once. It caused me a great deal of embarrassment, and I've not forgotten it.'

'What happened to that vessel?'

'It sank in a storm off the Shetlands.' Jurriaen's face tightened as he caught for a brief second the suspicion in Reyndert's sliding glance.

'Oh.' Again that gap-toothed smile. 'How annoying for you. Well, now you will be sharing the responsibility with Jacobsson and de

Groot of getting an unsinkable ship off the slips sometime in the future.'

A thought struck Jurriaen. 'By the way, what happened to the shipwright whose place I'm taking?'

'He was killed—crushed by a falling beam.'

Jurriaen whistled through his teeth. 'It seems a truly ill-fated ship. If I had the choice of coming again, I tell you quite frankly that I'd have had no part of it!'

The following day Reyndert took Jurriaen to meet Masters Jacobsson and de Groot, and to see the *Wasa*. The sisters went with them, but were warned that they would not be allowed to go on board.

Lying at Skeppsholmen, not far from the Castle, the *Wasa* was already a sight to catch the breath, being of the remarkable length of a full two hundred feet. The two battery decks and the orlop deck were completed, but the maindeck still gaped at the sky, the struts of the double galleries of the afterpart, yet to be glazed, formed an open network of timbers. Along the sides of the ship a double row of gun-ports, still without covers, gave glimpses of those at work within the ship—craftsmen, journeymen, and assistants in every trade—while a swarm of struggling men, their shirts darkened by sweat, sought with the aid of pulleys to lower a sixteen foot column into its socket.

'I'd love to go on her!' Lysbeth declared as Jurriaen and Reyndert went up the swaying gangway and disappeared from sight.

'I suppose we'd be in the way.' Jacintha, resigned to waiting some little time, looked about for a place to sit down, and selected a low stock of deck timbers, but Lysbeth went rushing off to view the ship from another angle.

Jacintha did not see the man, tall, broad-shouldered, who came slowly down the stone steps nearby. He had seen her from the verge above, and he approached her leisurely, not through lack of eagerness, but in a desire to observe every detail of the appearance of the slender girl, who sat with hands resting lightly upon each other in her lap, feet together beneath the folds of her full almond-green skirts, and whose profile was turned to him, shaded by the wide brim of her plumed hat.

'Juffrouw den Hartogh,' he said with a bow. 'Welcome to Sweden.'

She turned her head sharply as her eyes flashed up to meet that searching, dark blue gaze. Instantly she was aware of a fluttering panic, which she thought could only be due to the association of that look with the long-ago winter accident, but nevertheless she straightened up abruptly where she sat, bringing her hands up with wrists crossed to rest against her breasts in an oddly defensive attitude. 'Captain Halvarsen!'

109

'You remember me!'

She had not remembered that his voice was deep and beautiful. Neither had she retained the memory of the broad brow, the large, handsome nose and the thrusting chin that balanced those remarkable heavy-lidded eyes and well-cut mouth. She judged him to be about thirty, a man to be wary of, formidable as the country that had brought him forth, and the persuasive charm of his delighted smile had no effect on the steely tension of her tilted head and taut body.

'I was conscious for a few moments. That was all,' she said hastily.

His thick fair hair had lighter sun-streaks through it, and he kept his hat, which he had doffed, still in his gloved hand as he sat down beside her, resting his arm on his knee. 'I was so afraid that I'd been completely erased from your mind.'

His attitude towards her was easy and relaxed, as though they had shared some long relationship instead of the briefest contact, and she was irrationally annoyed that he should be so completely oblivious of the disappointment she had suffered as a result of that collision on the ice. Moreover he seemed little surprised to find her so far from home.

'I must tell you that it was entirely due to your sleigh rushing out at me that I missed making contact with someone that I particularly

110

wished to meet, and that—' she finished on a rush of words, 'caused me far greater distress than the aching head that kept me abed for several weeks!'

'What can I do to make amends?' He sounded genuinely concerned.

'It's too late for anything to be done now,' she said wearily, letting her shoulders rise and fall, and looked towards the *Wasa* where more planks were being carried aboard. 'You did enough in not leaving me either to freeze to death, or to be rough-handled by others, and for that I'm grateful. That was an end to it.'

'I trust not, Jacintha.'

Her face jerked round at him at the familiar use of her name, and her eyes narrowed slightly. 'Are you not curious to know how I came to be in Stockholm?'

'Mevrouw Pieterzoon informed me by letter of the date you would be leaving Amsterdam, and so allowing for good wind and weather I had expected you to be here now. But it was just chance and my good fortune that we should meet this morning—'

'Why should Saartje Pieterzoon write to you about me?' she demanded, an edge to her voice. She was baffled, and a little hurt that her friend should have taken such action without her knowledge.

'I asked her to let me know how you progressed after I left you in her care. Her

111

bulletins on your state of health and recovery were more than welcome.'

'I wasn't aware of them. She should have told me.'

He put out a hand, almost as though he would have covered one of hers in reassurance, but it hovered, and withdrew quickly under her affronted stare. 'Don't look so outraged, Jacintha. News of your guardian's arrival would have reached me soon enough through official channels—so it was inevitable that we should meet again. Lay no blame at the Mevrouw's door for doing what I requested of her. She could hardly refuse. Her husband received orders from me on behalf of my government to the value of many thousand guilders, and it would not have been politic for her to have disobliged me.'

A lightning shaft of suspicion came to Jacintha, making her consider a possibility that was so absurd that she dismissed it again. In any case there was no chance of further talk on the subject at that moment as Lysbeth came running back, her black hair tossing away from her excited face, one hand holding the ribbons of her hat, and her rosy skirts a-flutter.

'I've never seen such a ship—' She stopped as Axel rose to greet her, and her eyes widened with surprise when she heard who he was. Then with her insatiable, and yet guileless curiosity she proceeded to ask him a flood of questions

112

about the *Wasa*, which he answered with authority, pointing out various sections of it to her, and when he mentioned the figurehead she interrupted him eagerly. 'What is it to be? Do tell me! An eagle? A warrior? Neptune himself?'

'Would you like to see it?' he asked, obviously thinking such interest deserved reward.

'Oh, yes!'

He turned to Jacintha, and offered her an arm as she rose. 'The woodcarvers' workshops are at Skeppsgaarden—close at hand. You'll see much to interest you.'

As they entered the first of the long, low-roofed timber buildings, Jacintha hung back slightly, her heart contracting with a renewed longing for Constantijn. How often she had looked into the faces of the young carvers in the workshops of Amsterdam, rarely glancing at the work in progress, as she had searched for the man she loved.

'There's the figurehead!' Lysbeth exclaimed excitedly, spotting it at once, and accompanied Axel closely as he led the way to the far end of the workshop where a great leonine sculpture stood in shafts of sunlight, making a splendid sight against the sombre background of age-blackened walls. A master carver broke away from some other work in hand, leaving his assistants to continue with it, and came forward with a bow, his grey hair sticking damply to his sweaty forehead, his shirt dusty with woodchips, prepared to answer any questions.

Jacintha picked her way carefully across a floor thick with shavings, and stood feeling as dwarfed by Axel's height and build as she did by the immense pouncing lion, its mouth agape for the kill, that reared above her.

'It's magnificent!' Her gaze travelled over it, noticing the shield between its paws, and the two large curved rails over its head, which were ornamented with the helmeted heads of fearsome-looking warriors. On each side, symbolizing the Swedish King's link with mighty rulers of the past, was a row of Roman emperors.

'You like it, Juffrouw?' The master carver looked well-satisfied, and he slapped a work-scarred hand possessively on the lion's flank. 'I've worked on carvings for many ships, but I tell you that none will have seen the like of the *Wasa* when she sets sail in all her glory.'

'What wood do you use?' Lysbeth asked.

'Only oak—from the forests of Smaaland.'

'Show us some of the other carvings, Master Tijsen,' Axel requested, and they moved on to view the gunwales for the poop deck ornamented with Hercules figures, the contorted male and female heads that were to form console-like supports for the lower gallery, the caryatids in the form of tritons, and a host of fine reliefs on panels, many of which were finished and ready for painting and gilding, while others were still only drawn in charcoal on the block, or emerging in the first stages where the central figures had been set in, and the backgrounds reduced.

From that workshop they were taken into all the other turf-roofed buildings where the great sculptures for the stern were being made, all in the same vigorous, spirited, and often grotesque style, which made the figures and animals seem frighteningly alive, about to shout and roar and thunder their defiance from those grimacing and thick-fanged mouths. Jacintha found the visit fascinating, and lingered a little in awe before one piece and then another. Often she looked into the faces of those busy with tools and gouge, as though the habit of searching was still with her, and she received smiles, looks, and glances, and here and there an impudent wink.

But she made up her mind not to visit Skeppsgaarden again. She must accept that for the time being Constantijn was lost to her, and until the day came when Jurriaen decided to return to the Netherlands she must find some way to fill her thoughts and her time. Visiting such surroundings, seeing the carvers at work, hearing the tap of mallet, the whirl of grindstone, the rasp of file, would only make more unbearable a yearning that she must learn

115

to live with.

Axel escorted them back to the *Wasa*. There Reyndert came hurrying alone down the gangway, his hand held out in greeting long before he came near to Axel, his face creased up in an ingratiating smile.

'Captain Halvarsen! What a long time since we last met! I see you have made the acquaintance of our lovely young Dutch ladies. How well you look, sir! I can see by your tan that you have been many hours in the saddle. But then, when a man rides as well as you, sir, what better exercise can be taken? Tell me, what brought you to cast your observant eye over the *Wasa* today? Checking that all is going well, I suppose.'

His sycophantic garrulity had no effect on Axel, who simply answered in polite monosyllables when it was necessary, and only when an invitation proved to be forthcoming did a tiny glint show in his eyes.

'You must come and sup with us soon, Captain. I should like you to meet another new arrival to these shores—the guardian of these two beauties. Is he not a fortunate fellow? Why not tomorrow evening? What do you say?'

Axel looked directly at Jacintha, and then accepted. 'I should be delighted. Until then—your servant, Juffrouws—and Mynheer.' He turned, and walked back up the stone steps and was lost from sight amid passers-by.

116

Reyndert talked about Axel on the way home. It was Lysbeth who asked the questions, and although Jacintha listened she was very much absorbed in the bustle of the salty, sea-faring city of the waters that lay all about them. Fish in creels were being unloaded along the quays, making the cobbles wet, and there were sails and masts and bridges at every turn.

'Captain Halvarsen served with the army until he received a severe wound at the battle of Wallof when the Poles were defeated. Since then he has been entrusted with government duties, and has been abroad several times.'

'Is he well connected?' Lysbeth asked curiously. She had been impressed by him.

'Indeed he is—a cousin of the King's brother-in-law. Count Palatine John Casimir. The Captain was in the Count's entourage when the King accompanied them incognito to Berlin in the spring six years ago.'

'Why did the King do that?' Lysbeth asked.

'Travel incognito? Oh, there were political reasons. Then in Berlin he met Maria Eleonora, daughter of the Electress Dowager, who fell head over heels in love with him on sight without knowing who he was. He reciprocated her feelings, and brought her back to Sweden as his Queen.'

'How romantic!' Lysbeth exclaimed breathlessly. 'I must ask Captain Halvarsen if he was witness to their meeting. I've heard of

117

love at first sight, but never thought it possible.'

'Oh, it is!' Reyndert said roguishly, looking at her out of the corner of his eye.

Jacintha noticed with amazement that Lysbeth did not rebuff him, but giggled in a foolish way. Yet she knew her sister well enough to recognize the curl of contempt in the slight dilation of the delicate nostrils.

★   ★   ★

It was not to be a quiet evening as Jacintha had at first supposed. Reyndert in his position as liaison-representative between Dutch and Swedish was a person of some weight and importance in the community. Through the doors of his house, which also held his offices, there was a never-ending coming and going during the day, and his evenings were either taken up with light social duties, or else entertaining on a lavish scale those whom he considered it worth while to keep humoured and sweetened. At the supper to which Axel had been invited no less than two score other guests were to attend, and musicians were to play for dancing. Lysbeth was beside herself with excitement, and came darting into Jacintha's bedchamber to whirl about, her white tulip skirts swinging out, her rose velvet jacket a-flutter with lace.

'How do I look, Jacintha? Do you like my

118

hair like this? Would my other brocade slippers be better than these? Oh, if only I had some fine jewels to wear!' These last words were exploded on a moan as she came to a halt before the looking-glass, and trailed her fingertips down her throat to her full and creamy bosom.

'You look very fine, Lysbeth,' Jacintha answered, picking up her fan. She had chosen an apricot shot silk gown with a basqued bodice, and there were gold-gauzy ribbon knots entwined in her hair. She was not looking forward to meeting Axel again. She found him disturbing, and during the tour of the carvers' workshops she had been aware of his eyes on her all the time. There was a steel-like quality about the man, unbending, tenacious, and she had sensed a growing intensity of purpose towards herself that was both alarming and unwelcome. She decided to pay him little attention that evening, and make her indifference very obvious. She realized only too well that such an attitude could be an incitement and a challenge to such a man, but that was a risk she would have to take. In future his company should not prove too difficult to avoid.

'Good even, Jacintha.' He was waiting at the foot of the stairs, looking up at her as she descended, with that guarded, but dangerously elated expression in his eyes. His falling ruff reached the edge of his broad shoulders, and about his waist he wore the blue sash of the Royal household, its tassels glinting gold.

Mercy! How tall he is! she thought again, and suffered him to take her hand and lead her towards the salon where many of the other guests were already gathered.

The evening was hot and close, and even when supper was over the doors and windows still stood open wide to gardens that Reyndert had had laid out like a Dutch park with a fountain that looked faintly absurd against the frontier of black pines that stood at the lawn's end, warning of who knew what in the dark forest that stretched beyond.

Jacintha shivered as she looked towards it. 'Are there wolves in there?' she asked. She had danced for over an hour with various partners, but when Axel had sought to claim her again she had pleaded weariness. It had been a useless excuse, for he had promptly suggested that they should take a quiet turn in the garden as some of the other guests were doing, and sit down for a while.

'Oh yes,' he answered, amused at her nervousness. His arm was resting along the back of the seat behind her. She was sitting stiffly, her back very straight, the feathers of her fan rippling against her throat. 'But you'd not see them at this time of the year. It's in the winter that they're a great danger to travellers. I've had them howling around me many times

120

when I've been travelling between Stockholm and my estate that lies an hour's ride from here. It's an eerie experience suddenly to see their eyes burn red through the trees.'

'How horrible!' She hunched her shoulders in aversion. 'No wonder the forests here look so alarming.'

'That's only because you are so newly come from the wide open Netherlands. There are dark shades to this country, but much that is wild and beautiful too. Mountains and lakes and waterfalls—valleys so thick with flowers that their fragrance goes to your head like wine—and along the coast the islands and the skerries lie thick upon every inlet. Come!' He stood up, and held out his hand. 'It's just the hour to show you some gentler creatures that haunt the forests.'

She hesitated, but her curiosity was strong, and she rose, letting him take her hand in a firmer, more familiar grip than earlier that evening. They went along the path between the flower-beds, under the carefully contrived arches, and came to a low wall. Before she realized what was happening he had swept her up in his arms to lift her over it, holding her as he had done on that bleak, cold day in Amsterdam. But instead of setting her down immediately on the ferny ground on the other side, he looked lingeringly into her face. Then he bent his head and his lips, warm, dry, tender, touched hers briefly before he put her back on her feet again.

'You'll have to be very quiet,' he said calmly, as if the kiss had not happened, and held aside the branches for her as he led the way.

She was baffled by him, and looked from his broad back, which blocked her view when the way was narrow, to his finger and thumb that clasped her wrist like a bracelet. He obviously had not expected her to make any stupid fuss over the kiss, and it had been almost like a seal set with approval on some relationship that he seemed to imagine existed between them. She glanced about as they went deeper and deeper into the forest. It smelt fresh and green and ferny, but it was very dark, almost black in places; yet high above between the tree-tops the pale sky of the Scandinavian night held an almost liquid translucence. There was no sound now of the music from the house. Just a whispering of branches and grass, and the occasional snap of a twig underfoot.

'I hope you know your way back again,' she said, half in jest and half earnest. Then she was taken by surprise as he halted abruptly, glancing down over his shoulder at her as she came bumping into him.

'Would it matter?' His eyes were a-twinkle.

'Indeed! Yes! Of course.' She was flustered, and annoyed with herself for being so. She heard him give a quiet chuckle before he turned

122

about, and led her on again.

They came at last to a clearing that led away some distance up a hillside. 'This should be the place,' he said, and very gallantly he slipped off his sash to spread it over a dry old tree-trunk for her to sit upon, and then took his seat beside her. Nearby a stream gurgled and splashed, and all around them was a mist of pink and purple harebells. 'Are you learning not to fear the forest yet, Jacintha?' he asked.

She smiled, and leaned back a little, resting her weight on her hands just behind her. 'It's very peaceful.'

'You hear no chimes?'

'No.' She looked bewildered. 'Is there a church nearby?'

He shook his head, laughing. Then he swept his hand across the harebells, making them bounce back in a wild dance. 'They say that only those in love can hear these flowers ring their chimes.'

'But—' She bit back her protestation that the legend must be untrue. No one was more in love than she. Yet perhaps lovers had to be together to hear such magic music in their hearts.

'Yes?' he prompted.

'Have you ever heard them?' she asked evasively.

'Not yet.'

She turned the subject quickly. 'I may do a

series of flower sketches in the next few weeks. I'll include the harebell.'

'You are an artist then? Like your father?'

She flashed him a hard glance. 'So Saartje filled in all my background for you too!'

'Only while I stood with her at your bedside while we awaited the physician.'

She was slightly mollified, accepting his explanation, and she put her talent into perspective for him. 'I have little skill compared with my father. I believe him to have been a brilliant painter—somehow his inexhaustible vitality came through in his art. Lysbeth and I were allowed to keep a few of his drawings. Perhaps you would like to see them?'

'I should like that very much.'

She sighed heavily. 'I cannot help wishing that I could find some useful way to keep myself occupied. It seems as though we are to live under Mynheer Leeghwater's roof for some time. He has advised Jurriaen to buy land and build his own house, for it can always be sold when we leave this country again, and apparently rented apartments are hard to come by. But that means I shall have many hours of idleness on my hands.'

Before he could make some comment his watchful attention was caught by a shadow of movement in the distant trees. He touched her arm warningly, and put a finger to his lips. Then to her delight she saw emerging into the clearing a small herd of red deer, and they advanced as delicately as though weightless across the grassy slope. She held her breath, and in her excitement clutched his hand and held it to her, giving no thought to the other arm that he placed about her waist.

The deer came so near that she could hear the quiet champing of grass, and one stag rubbed his antlers vigorously against a nearby tree, making the branches shake. Then suddenly one hind, coming a little closer, scented the silent watchers in the shadows, and instantly the whole scene changed. With one accord the herd swung about, and went thundering away back up the hillside.

Jacintha sprang to her feet, and Axel with her. The last deer vanished from sight. 'That was wonderful!' she cried joyfully, and it was only then, as she spun about to face him, that she realized that she was within the circle of his arm. And she saw that this time it was to be no light and fleeting kiss, but one of passion and intense desire.

Any words that she had been about to speak were silenced. It was a kiss unlike any other she had ever known. This was no boy's awed and tender ardour, but the mouth of a man who knew how to awaken and inflame senses that set the heart pounding, and the blood racing. Yet with Constantijn filling her mind, a silent scream of protest made her so taut and unbending in Axel's arms that he was forced to become aware of it, and easing his grip upon her, he sought to reassure with softer loving of his lips. He was startled and disappointed when she thrust herself away from him with stiff and angry arms.

'We've stayed too long! We must return! For all we know the other guests may have left long since!' She darted back through the forest, sweeping aside the low branches, heedless of the brambles that caught and tore at her gown. But he had chosen the way there carefully, and in her blundering she found her feet squelching in wet and soggy ground, ruining the silk of her shoes. She plunged on, but slipped and fell to her knees. Then was up and on again. A cry escaped her as suddenly he loomed up in front of her.

'You're going in the wrong direction,' he said.

The house was full of lights, but the servants were clearing up, and the guests had all gone. She entered a side door, and ran upstairs to her bedchamber, leaving Axel to find his host having a last drink with Jurriaen in the library. There he thanked Reyndert, and made his departure.

Jacintha did not hear him go. She was examining her lips in a small hand-glass, amazed that such a kiss should leave no imprint.

126

CHAPTER SEVEN

In a turret room in the Castle of the Three Crowns the Countess Catherine, sister of the King, regarded her husband's cousin with curious interest. Shrewdly she suspected the reason why he was concerning himself with the affairs of a young Dutchwoman who had so recently come to these shores, but she was not going to let him know it yet.

'Why have you come to me about this matter?' she asked, lifting her pink feathered fan, and using it lazily. She had a disarming way of staring straight at a person when she talked, well aware of the power of her charm, and it was on her shoulders that much of the responsibility lay in smoothing the way between the ill-tempered, neurotic Queen and the long-suffering court.

Axel leaned forward eagerly in his chair. 'You are ever concerned for your fellow men—always an ear for a case of hardship, willing to intervene when misjustice is afoot, and I know how you sent your own retainers with food and supplies far afield in the bitter winter of last year when so many of the peasants were starving. Jacintha wants to fill her time in some purposeful way, and who better to advise her than you, my dear Catherine?'

'I declare that I could do with some advice myself at the moment as to how to comfort the Queen. She weeps incessantly while the King is away from home. Sometimes her tears flow for days on end, and she will not be comforted. She is as fearful of losing her husband to the arms of another woman as she is for his death in battle.'

'Then let her serve the Queen! Lighten her heart! Jacintha could read to her—teach the skill of drawing and painting—play Tric Trac with her—a thousand small services!'

Catherine shook her head. 'The Queen has her own German women round her, and has become so strange in her moods in the King's absence that often she will barely tolerate my presence. She makes no secret of her longing for her own country, and her loathing of Sweden and its people. She is both homesick and lovesick, and I tell you that the burden put upon all of us here at court is intolerable. Gustavus Adolphus is our well-loved King, but there will be a certain amount of selfish relief in our rejoicing when he comes home from the war to spend the winter with Her Majesty!'

'Then I'll not have Jacintha here in such depressing conditions. I must trust you to think of something else.'

'Are you in love with this girl, Axel?' she asked, her soft stare impassive.

He glanced quickly at her, knitting his brows, and gave a single quick nod as he shifted

128

in his chair, and sat back, swinging one long leg over the other. His gaze became abstracted as he rested an elbow on the arm of the chair, and he rubbed his chin thoughtfully. Catherine sensed that he was on the edge of confidence, and waited patiently.

'I cannot understand Jacintha,' he said at last. 'She's an enigma. Full of light and shadow. Talkative, laconic, gay, glowing, and sad in turn. There's passion in her, but damned up by some deep-rooted determination not to surrender to it. That's why I must take my time—she's not to be rushed, but it goes hard with me, Catherine.' There was a cynical flicker in his eye as he smiled across at her. 'I'm not a patient man.'

'Would you like my opinion, Axel?'

'Of course!'

'She sounds to me like a woman in love—with someone else.'

For a moment she wished she had not spoken with such candour, not suspecting that there were depths to his ardour. He had known so many women, and she had supposed this affair to be like any other. But his whole face had reflected his incredulous and furious dismay, and it was obvious that the possibility of a rival had not crossed his mind.

'She is not betrothed! No one was courting her in Amsterdam! I made enquiries about that.'

'That is no guarantee that she is not in love, Axel—but you do not need me to tell you that. Perhaps she met someone on the ship over.' Then, when he shook his head impatiently, refusing to consider such a possibility, she added: 'What of this young guardian that you were telling me about? Could it be he?'

'Oh, no.' He was very sure on that point. 'They tolerate each other, but I doubt whether there is any liking between them. He's a greedy, grasping fellow, who prefers to spend his leisure time at the gaming tables and with whores.' He lifted his head again, and his whole face had hardened inexorably. 'If she is mooning after some thick-headed Dutchman that she's left behind, it will go ill with her not to put him out of her mind.' Then he continued vehemently, seemingly trying to convince himself, his sanguine temperament taking over: 'But I'll not accept that you are right in your deduction. After all, you have not even met her yet!'

'That is true,' she said kindly, 'but I shall remedy that situation at the earliest possible moment.'

He rose quickly from his chair, and took up her hand to kiss it, his eyes raised to hers. 'Speak to her with favour on me, Catherine. I have known no love like this before.'

It had come as a pleasant surprise to Jacintha to find that her Dutch tongue was at home with many Swedish words, and realised that it would not be long before the language, which already had a familiar ring, would click into place with her. When she heard that French was the language of the court she gave it no thought, having no expectation of ever passing under the Swedish national emblem of three golden crowns that blazed above the entrance of the Royal Castle, and it was with astonishment that she received an invitation to wait on Countess Catherine Palatine at noon the following day.

'Why have I been invited?' Jacintha exclaimed, staring at the paper in her hand.

'Here! Let me see!' Lysbeth snatched it from her excitedly, and read it aloud. Then some of her exuberance went, lowering the tone of her voice. 'Why haven't I been included?'

Then the two sisters looked at each other in sudden comprehension. 'Axel!' they said in unison.

'Do you think he will be there too?' Lysbeth asked eagerly.

'I don't know,' Jacintha said slowly, torn between the hope of seeing a face familiar to her amid such awesome surroundings, and yet at the same time wishing that it could be anyone but Axel.

'What are you going to wear?' Lysbeth's thoughts had already turned to what she considered the most important aspect of the whole affair. The rest of that afternoon was

131

spent in Jacintha's bedchamber as every garment was taken from the closet, discussed, tried on, rejected, and tried on again. The final choice was a lime yellow jacket worn with a wide falling collar, and greyish-green taffeta skirt.

Reyndert insisted upon Jacintha having the use of his coach. He did not miss an opportunity to lavish favours on the two sisters, but whereas Lysbeth accepted them eagerly enough Jacintha avoided them, repelled by the man's obsequiousness, and wanting to be under no obligation to him in any way. But there was no getting out of being conveyed in the proffered transport. When she was ready to leave Reyndert stood waiting by the door to help her into the waiting vehicle himself, and it would have been churlish to have refused at that point. However, she could have covered the distance as speedily on foot, as on one of the narrow bridges there was confusion as a cart became jammed against the coach wheels, and the delay was considerable. At the Castle she dismissed the coachman, saying that she would walk back, and then entered its chill gloom.

It was with relief and a certain amount of surprise that Jacintha, rising from her curtsey, became aware that she and the Countess Catherine, were alone in the small, richly-furnished room.

'Sit down, Mademoiselle den Hartogh,'

Catherine said, indicating a chair on the opposite side of the chimney piece. 'I understand that your guardian is working with Masters Jacobsson and de Groot on the new *Wasa*. Have you been to see it yet?'

She had spoken in French, and was agreeably surprised when Jacintha answered her fluently, her Dutch accent too slight to blemish what was obviously a sound command of the language.

'I went the day after I arrived in Stockholm. It's going to be a very fine ship when completed—Captain Halvarsen took my sister and myself to see sculptures being carved at Skeppsgaarden.'

'You are here today because the Captain recommended you to me.'

'I did suppose that, Madame.'

Then Catherine, saying no more on that issue at the moment, encouraged Jacintha with further questions, leading her on to talk about her sister, her parents, and her home life in the little South Holland village. As Jacintha answered she could see in her mind's eye the humble house where she had known so much happiness, and it seemed to her that she could smell again the aroma of turpentine and paint that had ever lingered in its little rooms.

Catherine, listening closely, formed her own opinion of this young Dutchwoman that had attracted Axel so strongly. She had expected to find her a creature of exceptional beauty,

133

remembering others in the past, but here was a girl with little to commend her beyond good bones and fine colouring, small high breasts, and waist slender as a stem. How then had Jacintha managed to cast such a spell over Axel? He had described the incident of their meeting; so was it her very helplessness as she lay there on the ice that had aroused a latent romanticism in him, or was there something more? There was no doubt that the girl had a serenity of features that would appeal to a turbulent man like Axel, and yet there was a strength of will behind those wide, candid eyes. She would not be easily won.

Catherine had ordered a cold collation to be served with a light wine, and afterwards when they had eaten and the dishes had been removed, she decided that now she would explain what she had in mind. If, in spite of Axel's praise, Jacintha had proved unsuitable in her judgement, she would have simply dismissed the girl, and that would have been the end of the matter as far as she was concerned. But she liked Jacintha, and felt she had qualities that could be put to good use.

'Captain Halvarsen told me that you seek some useful way to employ your time. I have an idea to put to you, and although you would find what I have to suggest arduous and exacting at times, I feel you would be able to carry it out very well.'

'You arouse my interest and my curiosity, Madame.'

Catherine's hands were resting on the carved heads of lions which formed the arms of her chair, the jewels on her fingers casting little darts of prismatic light across the face of the girl who waited to hear what she had to say, undismayed by the warning.

'As you know, Mademoiselle, here in Sweden at the present time we are unable to raise the number of stone-masons, wood-carvers, iron-workers, and many other craftsmen that are essential to our growing economy, and therefore we must draw them from other countries. Many of these men come intending never to return to their own lands again, and they bring their wives and families with them, and often aged parents and other dependents. German workers predominate, and one of Her Majesty's ladies-in-waiting, who is from Berlin, interests herself in the well-being of her humbler fellow countrymen. It occurred to me that it would be sensible to have a feminine link with the families of Dutch workers, who—although fewer in number—are nevertheless an integral part of our community. Would you consider being this contact?'

'I would indeed! What duties should I perform?'

'Simply to visit each Dutch homestead in turn, see that the children are being cared for, and to report any case of extreme hardship to me. Accidents are frequent in the workshops, mines, and shipyards, and often there is dire need among families, some of them barely able to speak a word of Swedish, when the bread-winner is incapacitated for weeks, and even months on end. There are religious orders who see that the poor get fed, but they rarely look beyond those able to cluster at the gates, and word of individual cases of distress must be conveyed to them.'

'I cannot thank you enough, Madame, for giving me the chance to be of service in this way!' Jacintha exclaimed enthusiastically.

'Are you fond of children?'

'Yes, Madame. I've heard that you are blessed with a young family.'

Catherine smiled. 'They are my greatest joy. Our son, Charles Gustavus, is just four years older than the little Princess Christina, whom I love as dearly as if she were my own.' Then a thought occurred to her. There was a little extra favour that lay in her power to grant. 'Would you like to see the Princess? It is the hour for her to be taken from her nursery to spend a little time with the Queen.'

'I would indeed, Madame.'

It seemed to Jacintha that the Castle was a gloomy setting in which to grow up, dark and sombre, the chill of grey stone hanging in the air like the breath of winter. Many of the carvings were grotesque enough to frighten a small child, and the tapestries, magnificent though they were, depicted the more alarming mythological scenes with flame-blowing dragons, and hideous gorgons. At the foot of a wide flight of stairs, Catherine indicated that they should wait.

'She will be coming any minute now.'

As Catherine stood there her thoughts went back to a day eighteen months before when she had come down that staircase with a slow tread, full of trepidation, for it had fallen to her to break the news to her brother that his new-born child was not a boy as he had already been informed, but a daughter, a small girl so covered in hair as to be almost ape-like in appearance. None dared to tell him of the mistake that had been made, and she had gone with a sad and heavy heart to put an end to his rejoicing that he had his longed-for son at last. Never would she forget that moment when she broke the news, or how he had reacted, understanding how deep was her compassion for him. Putting his arms about her, he had said gently: 'Let us offer thanks to God, my sister. I hope this girl will be as worthy as any son to me. May God protect her, since He has granted her to me.' Then he had ordered all the ceremonies that were performed only for the first-born Prince. It was a tragedy that the Queen had no room in her heart for anyone but

137

the King, and was jealous of their only child that he loved so dearly. Not every day would she suffer the little princess to be brought into her sight. It was a daily ordeal never knowing whether she would shriek out in a fury that she did not want the brat brought near her, or whether she would snatch her up, and hug and rock her, dousing her with those tears that burst forth like a spring from a mountainside.

'Here comes the little Princess,' Catherine said to Jacintha, looking upwards with affection at the child that came toddling along the gallery above, clutching at her nurse's hand. She was fair-skinned, large-eyed, elaborately dressed in cinnamon velvet with a thickly beaded bodice, with a garlanded cap on her brown curls, and a musical toy hung on a gold chain around her neck, the little bells tinkling as she trotted a little unsteadily towards the head of the stairs.

'Pick her up now,' Catherine said warningly as the nurse made no attempt to lift the child.

'Her Majesty has ordered that the Princess Christina must walk everywhere to strengthen her legs, your Grace,' the nurse, a solemn-faced woman, answered guiding the child's hand to that part of the carved bannisters that she could reach, and obediently one small foot hung suspended over the drop to the next stair.

'No! No!' Catherine flung out a protesting hand, and took a step forward with a hiss of silk. 'Christina! Stay!'

But the child, eager to master this new venture, stepped down, her baby grip immediately losing contact with support as she lost balance, and spun like a top from the nurse's strong clasp of her other hand.

'Enough!' Catherine stormed. 'Take up the Princess this instant!'

The nurse, startled by the fury of the order, bent to obey, but even as she loosened her hold to take the child by the underarms a great grey rat, its feet making a hideous scratching sound in its rushing flight from the gallery, came bounding downwards past her skirts. The woman screamed out, throwing up her hands, and the Princess, tottering, plunged head first down the stairs.

Jacintha hurled herself up the flight to break the tumbling fall, but was too late to prevent a descent of at least six stairs before she caught her. The child had gone deathly white, drawing in her breath as though she could never release it again, her eyes rolling up to show the whites, her back arched.

Then Catherine was there, lifting her swiftly but competently from Jacintha's arms, just as a great bellow broke from the child, and the tormented sobbing that followed mingled with the continued screaming of the nurse on the stairs, whose fear of the rat had now changed to a greater terror of what had befallen. From all directions people had come running, and the double doors directly below the flight, which led to the Queen's apartments, burst open to let forth a swarm of dwarfs, midgets, and others so grotesquely deformed that Jacintha, in the midst of her concern for the child, whose shoulder appeared to be broken, stared in disbelief as they rushed up to close around and hinder Catherine's hastening down with Christina in her arms, many of them gibbering, their gaudy clothes accentuating their bizarre appearance.

'Out of my way!' Catherine thundered, and the Queen's own women, who had come flocking in their wake, thrust them aside with brutal cuffs. Then, as Catherine reached the foot of the stairs, the Queen herself came sweeping through the doors, her fine-looking face distraught with terror at what she might find.

'What happened? Is she much hurt? Dear God, how white she is!' She would have snatched at the child, but Catherine swung her sobbing burden away protectively.

'Have a care, Madame! She is injured, but not dangerously, I trust.'

'Give me my baby!' the Queen shouted hysterically, and snatched Christina from her sister-in-law's arms. The child shrieked out in agony, one little arm swinging unnaturally, and was borne away by her mother, who was screaming out for physicians to be fetched, closely followed by Catherine, and then the whole strange retinue vanished beyond the doors again.

Those left in the hallway were all asking each other how it had happened, and had anyone witnessed the occurrence, but the nurse had vanished, and Jacintha, trembling with reaction, remained silent. She set off to make her way from the Palace, and lost herself in a maze of corridors until a servant guided her to the main entrance hall.

It was a relief to get out into the sunshine, and the air was clean and salty, a light wind blowing from the sea. She walked the considerable distance back to Reyndert's residence, careless of the dust that whitened her skirt-hems, thankful for the exercise, and the chance to think over the extraordinary events of the past four hours. Most bewildering of all was the reason for the appearance of a wharf-rat at that particular moment. Had some unseen hand released it from a trap? There had been attempts on the Princess's life before, and had the little one fallen the full flight from such a height it was doubtful whether she would have survived. Jacintha shuddered at the thought, and wondered if inadvertently she had been instrumental in thwarting yet another attempt on the life of the King's heir by his enemies.

In the turmoil and throughout the interrogations that followed Christina's fall, which threatened to leave one of the child's shoulders permanently ill-formed, Catherine did not forget her promise to Jacintha, and sent a fine mare for her use, and word that escort would be available at any time. Jacintha sought Reyndert Leeghwater's assistance in locating the Dutch families, but although he knew those of wealth and position the humbler folk, such as she wished to seek out, were unknown to him, and he could only indicate on a chart the poorer quarters of the city, and the primitive dwellings clustered near the yards and dotted about in the forest, where they might be found.

The next morning she set off accompanied by a servant wearing the Princess Catherine's own livery, but the fellow's grand appearance struck awe into those whom she visited, and her own Dutch accents failed to put them at their ease. Yet she did find one family badly handicapped by having taken in two orphaned children when both parents had fallen ill and died. There were grandparents in Haarlem, but no money available for the repatriation of the children. Jacintha saw that this was a matter that she could easily arrange by consultation with one of the many sea-captains that came to Reyndert's house, and promised to write herself to Haarlem. On the way home she decided to dispense with an escort, except when she went further afield. In the meantime she would go alone to visit those who lived within a radius that she could visit easily either on foot or horseback.

She had hoped to interest Lysbeth in the work she was undertaking, but her suggestion of involvement was greeted with a grimace of disdain.

'I've more entertaining ways in which to pass my time, Jacintha.'

'Have you forgotten how glad we would have been of help and shelter that night we had to sleep under the stars in Amsterdam?' Jacintha asked levelly. 'Think how much worse to be in distress in a foreign country.'

Lysbeth shrugged carelessly. 'Do as you wish—but don't expect me to come dragging after you!'

Jacintha's contact with the Castle, which looked as though it were to be permanent, had aroused an intense jealousy in Lysbeth, and she sought to outshine her sister in other ways. It was not proving difficult. Her dark, brooding looks pronounced the restless, untamed side of her nature, and drew men to her in a way that she could not have dreamed possible within the narrow confines of their limited social activities in Amsterdam. Here in Reyndert Leeghwater's house things were very different, which was to Lysbeth's great satisfaction.

She knew how to display her charms to advantage, setting off her lovely throat and well-shaped shoulders with the fashionable décolletage, and choosing rich, strong colours for the materials of her gowns, which accentuated the indigo-black glossiness of her luxuriant hair. Although her devotion to Jurriaen was unchanged, she began to flirt and entice, enjoying her new-found power, and her easy, spontaneous behaviour encouraged those who danced attendance on her to hope that the promise of her glances would be fulfilled the moment that the opportunity arose. She teased and tantalized, was ignored by Jurriaen, watched anxiously by Jacintha, and lusted after by Reyndert.

CHAPTER EIGHT

Jacintha came downstairs dressed ready for the ride that was to take her far south of Stockholm. She had heard of a case of extreme distress, and felt that she must go personally to see what was to be done about the matter. Although it was early in the day there were a number of people waiting in the hall to see Reyndert on official business, and she was surprised to see Axel among them.

He rose from one of the chairs set back against the wall as she appeared, and came forward. 'Good day, Jacintha. I asked the Countess Catherine to allow me to be of service at any time in the task that you've undertaken. So today I have come to escort you myself on your journey instead of entrusting the safety of your person to a servant. Shall we go?'

There was little she could say within earshot of those crowding the hall, and had no choice but to accept graciously.

'That was considerate of you. I understand the way is long and covers difficult terrain.'

They rode out through the south gate of the city, Jacintha averting her eyes from the mouldering heads that were mounted on it, and then the air was filled with the summer scent of hay-making. It was a warm soft day with enough breeze to ripple the fast ripening cornfields, and everywhere peasants were at work. Then gradually the little turf-roofed timber-walled farmsteads, clustered together for protection when the terrible winters descended, became more sparse, and the countryside stretched out in a wild and beautiful tangle of forest, river and hillside. Sometimes the way was so narrow that Axel had to ride ahead of her, but he was quick to drop back and ride stirrup to stirrup with her again. Once an elk, its antlers branched heavy and wide, surveyed them from high on a slope, and frequently ptarmigan rose up from the grass with a noisy beating of wings and whirled away to become distant specks above the treetops.

They talked as they rode. She had put all

145

thought of that throbbing kiss firmly from her, and was relaxed and content to enjoy the day. There was nothing in his glance, voice or actions to suggest that he had given the little encounter a second thought, and their conversation, among other topics, dealt with the war that showed signs of slowly gathering momentum, in spite of the lulls, often lengthy, that followed the outbursts of battle.

'The Hapsburg emperor is already calling General Wallenstein his admiral of the Baltic and the oceanic seas,' Axel said with some derision. 'He's far too previous! With the *Wasa* and the three other men-o'-war being added to our navy Wallenstein will meet his match. But firstly he must get possession of several Baltic seaports to serve as bases for his own fleets, and I cannot see an old Hanseatic city like Stralsund surrendering without a struggle. It may well call upon us for aid, and then we'll really get to grips with the General. It would give us a footing on German soil at the same time.' Then he did cast a sidelong glance at her. 'It's fortunate for us that our countries are allied, Jacintha, or else we should not be riding together on such a perfect day.'

But she said nothing in reply, and kept her eyes on the way ahead.

They broke their journey to sit on the bank of a churning river, its spray silvering the air, and eat the cold capon, fruit, cheeses and bread that

146

had been packed into the saddlebag. Axel had brought a flagon of wine, and it was pleasant to picnic amid the rainbow flutter of butterflies, and to rest for a while. He lay propped on one elbow beside her as she sat, her skirts a bunched yellow-striped cloud over her legs which she had drawn under her, drinking the wine that he had poured for her out of a pewter mug.

'Jurriaen Haaring is remarkably young to have authority over you and your sister,' he said curiously. 'How did it come about?'

She told him, and because it was still and peaceful and he was listening without moving as much as a finger she described in detail the evening she arrived with Lysbeth at Jurriaen's house in the Nez, and confided her misgivings at committing herself and her sister to Jurriaen's charge, and the stipulation that she had made.

'Have you had reason to suppose that your original fears were well grounded?' he asked at length.

'Oh, yes!' she answered on a fierce note of bitterness. 'I would not have found myself in Sweden if it had not been for my signature upon that document!'

This time it was his turn to remain silent. He rose, and dropped forward onto one knee as he started to repack the saddlebag. She sensed the sudden strain in the atmosphere as though he were holding back much that he wished to say. She would be thankful when they reached their destination, and then the return journey home could begin, making an end to the day. There was too much silent conflict between herself and this man, and these lapses into a kind of amiable armistice deceived neither of them. A sharp word, a challenge, and even a sudden silence could be enough to inflame a situation as though tinder had been put to the dry summer grass that surrounded them. She swung herself up into her side-saddle before he could move to assist her, and did not glance again in his direction until the soft creak of leather told her he had mounted his horse beside her.

'I do not wish to stop long at this farmstead we are to visit,' she said, thinking that if they did not come upon it soon then it would be late at night before they saw Stockholm again.

He shrugged, and moved slightly ahead of her to find a safe place to cross the river.

'It may not be easy to get away without some delay. Visitors are made much of on these lonely farms, and it is considered discourteous to plunge into business without some social preliminaries.'

It was mid-afternoon before they came over the crest of a hill, and saw the farmstead set in a valley below. Walls of stout stakes surrounded it, and the house formed part of a square with the barn, byres, and outhouses. In the surrounding fields peasants were hay-making, but the frenzied barking of watch-dogs made everyone pause and straighten up from their labours, shading their eyes to watch the two riders approaching at a steady, unhurried pace. One burly man detached himself from the others, and came slowly forward to meet them. Three young men, their pitch-forks catching the sunlight, dropped into procession behind him, and when he stopped they formed a small phalanx around him. There could be no doubt that they were his sons, for all possessed looks that were a mere variation on the older man's heavy features and vulgar breadth of nose. They looked rough men, coarse and insensitive, but it was hard to reconcile their simple, hard-working appearance with the brutal tale that a traveller had brought to her of a little boy, whom he had been told was Dutch, chained up with the dogs on this isolated farm.

'God dag!' The farmer called out his greeting in genial tones, but stood with his feet set apart, huge hairy-backed hands linked in a belt from which a thick-handled knife hung in a leather sheath. Axel answered cheerily and dismounted, leading his horse and hers by the reins to cover the last remaining stretch of rough grass. Names were exchanged, the farmer being Karl Karlsen, and although the conversation was in Swedish Jacintha had become sufficiently attuned to the language to

149

follow the gist of it without much difficulty, although speaking it still presented problems.

'Have you come far?' Karl Karlsen enquired. He addressed himself to Axel, for in his world the women were subservient and without importance, except in the bearing of sons.

'All the way from Stockholm.'

'Then your news will be more than welcome. No traveller has passed this way for a month or more, and then bound for the city, and not from it. Come into the house, and have some refreshment. How goes the war? Is it true that Oxenstierna thinks himself the next ruler of Sweden? And what of the King himself? The last I heard was that he had been wounded on campaign.'

Jacintha, who would have made through her interpreter a simple outright request to see the Dutch boy and take him away if the allegations proved to be true, realized that Axel had come with her for the very good reason that he had suspected that she might find herself in a situation that could be beyond her powers to handle. Yet she was irritated by the direction of his full attention to the uncouth peasant who took no heed of her presence, hawking and spitting, and scratching himself under the armpits. It was obvious she had been relegated to the ranks of his own womenfolk, which was akin to slavery, judging by the way they were hauling cart-loads of hay. Two of them, no

150

doubt his wife and daughter, had stopped work, and were running past in an abject, servile manner to rush ahead and get food upon the table. The three sons fell away, returning to the hayfields, and Axel continued to lead Jacintha's mount on through the gates of the farmstead. There the farmer did take the horses into the stable, but it was Axel who helped Jacintha down from the saddle.

The farmhouse was very barren and primitive, consisting of one great living-room, which held two vast wall-beds, a long table, and benches, and an adjoining kitchen where a clatter of pans told that the women had lost no time in starting preparations for the meal. Karl invited Axel to sit down on the bench, flung himself into the great chair that stood at the head of the table, and thumped a fist in summons for a jug of ale to be brought.

The daughter came running with it, and poured it into two wooden tankards, which the men raised to each other. '*Skaal!*'

'Am I not to be offered anything?' Jacintha said icily to Axel, speaking in Dutch. She still stood just inside the doorway, making her isolation obvious.

'The women will offer you their best wine in a moment, Jacintha,' he answered, his eyes telling her that it was not his wish that she should have to suffer these customs.

'Eh? What's this? A foreign tongue!' Karl

had twisted about to stare at her under his over-hanging bushy brows.

'This lady is from The Netherlands,' Axel explained.

'Is she? Well, I've a crazy little Dutch devil on my hands that no amount of booting seems to improve.' With that he turned back to Axel again as though the subject were dropped.

'Where is he?' Jacintha asked in her halting Swedish. But Karl had not heard, and then the girl came with a wooden cup of wine, which Jacintha took from her with a smile. The girl blushed shyly, and hurried away to the kitchen. Deliberately Jacintha went across and sat down on the bench beside Axel. He put out a hand under the table to take hers consolingly, but she snatched it away.

The talk bored her. So much was spoken at a pace too swift for her to catch, and it seemed as if the meal was not to appear until all had come in from the fields. To judge by the slicked-down hair of the men all had washed themselves in a stream before coming indoors, but they had put the same sweat-stained clothes back upon their bodies, and the air became heavy and acrid. But the Dutch boy did not appear.

'Are we to sit here forever?' she demanded fiercely to Axel when the opportunity to speak arose under the noise of other voices.

'A state of patriarchy exists on these farms.

These farmers are very proud and stubborn men. Karl would take it as a great personal insult if we did not accept hospitality of his house, and you'd get no favours granted. Unless it was a knife in the ribs for me,' he added dryly. 'So shall we stay?'

Her eyes had darkened with alarm, and she nodded reluctantly. 'But it will be morning before we get back to Stockholm.'

'Oh, we'll have to sleep here,' he said casually. 'We couldn't set off after all the drinking that will be going on here tonight.'

She sat stunned, talk flowing about her as wooden platters and mugs were set on the table with horn spoons, and short knives with dangerous-looking blades. These turned out to be for cutting great chunks of dried and salted lamb off the bones, and for spearing the most succulent pieces of pork that turned up in a thick stew, which everybody else but Jacintha devoured with every show of gravy-dribbling enjoyment.

The feasting continued for two hours, and then all the platters were cleared away, and the drinking began. A vast wooden bowl, painted in vivid colours, filled with some special brew, was handed round for all to drink from. Round and round it went, and the company became noisier and more boisterous. A competition started amongst the men as to which of them could kick hardest the massive centre beam that

153

spanned the room, and those that missed fell flat on their back with a force that would have broken the bones of less stalwart men. Axel ripped off his jacket, and competed with the rest of them. Someone had started to play a primitive wailing fiddle, and feet thundered on the floor in dancing of tremendous enthusiasm and little grace, and went spilling out on to the grass before the house.

Jacintha, who had been seized about the waist by one of the sons, was whirled about in the throng, and if it had not been for the reason why she was there being uppermost in her mind she would have surrendered to the spontaneous merriment.

Axel came bounding outside with the rest of the men, and claimed her for himself, leading her in a dance in which all the girls were lifted high by their partners and soundly buffed at the end of it, but even as he snatched her to him she caught sight of a pitifully thin child, all eyes and bones, peeping cautiously round the corner of a byre at the shrieking dancers.

'There he is!' she cried. Before Axel could stop her she had rushed towards the boy, calling to him in Dutch, holding out her arms. But the child, giving her a look of terror, turned about and ran as fast as his thin little legs could take him, and when she came round to the back of the byre he was nowhere to be seen. There were a dozen doors through which he might

154

have darted, and a farm clutter of carts and bales and barrels that would have provided innumerable hiding-places. 'Where did he go?' she cried in despair as Axel came up to her.

'You'll not find him now,' he said. 'Come back.'

She turned on him in fury. 'I didn't come here to take part in a carousal, but to claim a child! Did you see him? He has been starved!'

He seized her by the arms. 'I've talked to Karl about him. The boy's mother is dead, and the father brought him here while seeking work, but absconded, leaving him behind. He could have settled down with the other children—after all, one more mouth makes little difference on a farm of this size—but he behaved outrageously. Breaking everything he could get hold of! Letting the sheep free! Upsetting churns of milk! The more they punished him the worse he became!'

'Did they withhold food from him too?' she demanded angrily.

'No, but he will no longer come into the house, and hides away for days sometimes, living on what he takes from the pigs' troughs. They think him no longer sane.'

'How terrible! I'll not leave without him!'

'You may have to. By chasing him like that you could have frightened him off from coming back for a week or more.'

'I'll search all night.'

155

'That you shall not do. Be patient. Leave it to me.'

'You!' she exclaimed with scorn, fiercely angry that he had not warned her at once of the boy's nervousness, but had swung her about in a merry dance as though it were a Mayday and their only duty to enjoy themselves. 'What could you do?'

He was exasperated by her scorn, and more than a little inflamed by the large amount of home-made brew that he had consumed. 'I brought you all the way to Sweden by pulling every string in my power, so by comparison this should be a small problem for me to settle!'

She stared at him, appalled by what he had said. The faint suspicion that had crossed her mind the day they had met by the *Wasa*—which she had dismissed as being too absurd to contemplate—was true after all!

'You caused that invitation to work on the *Wasa* to be sent to Jurriaen!'

'There are few shipwrights who would not have leapt at such an opportunity, and I had his background investigated. He's an enterprising young man of no mean talent when he exerts himself. Of course he has his weaknesses, but there was no reason to suppose that these would seriously hinder his ambitions for advancement and position, ensuring a very high standard of work, in the present circumstances.'

'Why Jurriaen out of so many others?'

'Can you not guess, Jacintha?'

'No!' Her exclamation of denial held her whole rejection of the only possible reason.

He moved closer to her, still holding her arms, and his whole body was pressed against hers. 'I wanted you here.'

'How did you know I'd come?' she cried wildly.

'I had it stressed that he would be expected to bring his dependents and settle here for some number of years at least. In any case, I knew you'd have no choice—Mevrouw Pieterzoon said that he enjoyed his domination over both you and your sister, and kept you with him like finches in a cage.'

'There was no cause to uproot us from our own land!'

'I could not win your love with the whole of the North Sea lying between us.'

'My love?' she echoed incredulously. Then she laughed, harsh, unhappy laughter that made the cords stand out on her throat, her shoulders hunched forward as she hugged her bitter mirth to her.

His face darkened and congested, and an intense muscular contraction of his forehead showed how difficult it was for him to keep his temper under control. 'I fail to understand your amusement!'

'I think you're mad!' she declared hoarsely. 'You did not know me! You knew nothing

157

about me, except what a gossiping friend chose to tell you, and yet in your monstrous conceit you thought you had only to bring me here, and I should find you irresistible! Well, I don't!' She tried to jerk away from him, but he continued to hold her hard. 'I could never love you! Nor anyone else in this country! I love someone else, and I shall go on loving him until the day I die! You've gone to a great deal of trouble all to no avail, and I've been uprooted from the only place in the world that I would be!'

Then she seemed to crumble under the impact of her own words, her head dropping forward to hide the sudden gush of tears to her eyes, which she struggled to keep back.

'Jacintha.' He spoke softly, fearful of the damage he had done to the relationship that he had been hoping to build up and nurture until he had roused in her a passion equal to his own. Cautiously, when she did not move or rebuff him further, her bowed forehead resting against his chest, he put up his hand to cup her head, and then stroked down the long flow of her soft hair, seeking to soothe and reassure. With all the sensitivity of a lover he knew how far she had gone from him, and yet still he hoped to coax her back again.

He remembered how he had first looked upon her lying on the ice with a strange kind of recognition, certain that here was the woman he had sought through a maze of other loves, and when she had opened her eyes to him he had been almost expecting to see the same ignited spark in hers. He had formulated his plans about bringing her to Sweden even before he had sailed from Amsterdam, and it was still inconceivable to him that he should have been rejected out of hand. Desire for her had given him no peace, and he had dreamt of her at night as if he were still a lovesick boy. All the love and tenderness that was in him came into his voice as he spoke to her again, his fingers moving towards her jawline to raise her face slowly upwards by his palm under her chin. 'Whatever lies in the past is over, Jacintha. Let me show you what love can mean.'

She lifted her glittering lashes with a sudden sweep, and her eyes were hard and cold as if part of her were dead. 'Leave me alone,' she said with a shivering, deadly edge to her words that ended all hope.

Then like some nightmarish world of trolls descending upon them, the rollicking dancers with shrieks and shouts came bounding between them to snatch them away from each other, and into a wild dance that neither wanted to join, but were shoved and pushed into the stamping, roisterous pattern of the steps. When it ended everybody collapsed on the grass to rest, and it was obvious that at last an awareness of the lateness of the hour, including the thought of work on the morrow, was putting an end to the festivities.

Karl stood up from the wooden bench where he had been watching the proceedings with a pipe, and over the rim of a tankard. Everybody cheered as he reeled unsteadily, and lifted his arms as he addressed them. 'This has been a memorable evening, and we are honoured that these folk from Stockholm have shared food and drink with us. Axel has asked one favour of me, and although the reason for it defeats me I'm happy to indulge the whim of his woman, who wants to take the Dutch boy back to Stockholm with her.' There were murmurs of incredulous surprise, and all looked towards Jacintha, who was kneeling on the grass, sitting back on her heels, beside the youth that had been partnering her in the last dance. 'T'would be better if Axel proved himself the man that he is, and gave her a babe of her own to worry about!' Gusts of bawdy laughter greeted this remark, and more followed with some cheering when he added coarsely: 'There's a good hard bed in our guestroom—let's hope they take advantage of it this night!'

Jacintha cared nothing for what they said. The boy was hers to take away. The only disquieting note had been struck by the implication that she was expected to share a bed with Axel that night.

'So let's conduct our guests to their quarters,'

Karl continued, giving a wide sweep of his arm—which made him stagger back a step—towards a flight of rough steps that led to the upper floor of an ancient timber storehouse. 'Then the rest of you hunt out the boy. Let's not lose this chance to be well rid of him in just cause!'

Everybody scrambled to their feet. Jacintha was seized by the wrist, and jerked up from the grass to be bundled with Axel at the head of a procession towards the steps. There she had no choice but to mount them, all way of escape blocked, and after one backward glance over her shoulder at the grinning, ale-flushed faces, the leering eyes of the men, she darted up and along the narrow gallery into the sloping-eaved room that topped the whole storehouse.

It smelt mealy from the corn stored below, and in spite of the pale night outside it was gloomy with dark shadows where old painted chairs and other furniture discarded from the house were arranged in a disorderly fashion; under the tiny horn-glazed window stood an ancient wedding chest bearing the date 1550. But the bed dominated the room. It must have been assembled there, for it was as large as those in the farmhouse itself, and spread with a quilt woven in every colour. The door opened, and she spun about as Axel entered, bending his tall head to avoid the low frame. He pulled the door, which opened outwards, closed to behind him, shooting in the wooden bolt, and then straightened up as he turned to face her, tossing aside the jacket thrown over one shoulder that had been handed to him on the steps. There was no more tenderness in his eyes.

'So we are to spend this night together, Jacintha.'

'I'm not getting into that bed!' She backed away as he took a few steps towards her. He shrugged, and began to unfasten his cuffs. His falling collar, already loosened during the dancing, showed his hirsute chest, and she gave a gasp as he pulled the shirt over his head.

'You're not undressing!' she exclaimed, outraged.

He glanced towards her. 'I've no intention of sleeping in my clothes.' Dropping his shirt on a chair, he went across to pour water from a wooden ewer into a bowl. His back was very powerful, the muscles rippling, but was marred by the violence of a great puckered, purple scar scored deep into the shoulder of his sword-arm, which explained why he had been reassigned by his sovereign to civil duties at home instead of those that he had previously carried out on certain foreign battlefields.

'You don't have to stay here!' she protested indignantly. 'Sleep in the barn! In the hay! There are plenty of other places!'

He went on splashing in the bowl. 'It would

look a little strange if I reappeared now. These are very moral people, and they would not have put us together if they had not believed us to be betrothed. Then you would have had to share one of the beds in the farmhouse with six other young women and a couple of children—while Karl and his wife snored behind the bed-curtains of the other—and I should have been in the stable-loft with some of the men. Neither of us is used to such overcrowded conditions, and I would say that this is to be much preferred.'

'Did you tell them we were betrothed?' she asked suspiciously.

He reached for a towel to dry himself, rivulets of water running down his face and body. 'No. And now you have made it very plain to me that we never shall be.' He paused, lowering the towel as he listened, a questioning frown on his face. 'What's that din outside?'

She went to the narrow window, and rested her face against the horn-pane as she put an eye to a crack to look out. 'They're running all over the place with ropes and sticks,' she said wonderingly. Then she swung round, pressing her back against the wall, her face distraught. 'They must be chasing the boy!' she cried in horror. 'Like a fox! Or a hare!'

He compressed his lips in distaste, but whether at the chase or the boy she was not sure. 'It seems to me we should have brought a cage with us. What are you going to do with the lad when you get him to Stockholm?'

She moved to sit on the edge of the wedding chest, turning away from him when after pulling off his riding-boots he started to unbuckle his belt.

'I'll have to keep him in our apartments in Reyndert's house. Lysbeth is fond of children, and she'll help me look after him.'

'I cannot see Leeghwater welcoming such a child under his roof. He has too many fine works of art that he has brought from the Netherlands. What would you do if the boy flung an ink-pot at one of those landscapes?'

'I don't know,' she said helplessly. 'It never occurred to me that he would be so wild and undisciplined.'

'I think I can take him off your hands—not that I'll let him near my house in Stockholm, but I've a good-hearted warden and his wife on my estate at Halversensgaard. They've taken in every other kind of stray from time to time, and I'm certain they would find a place in their home for this child.'

'Oh, thank you!' She twisted about involuntarily in a rush of gratitude. He was padding towards the bed at the end of the long shadowy room. Like a pale statue that had become warm flesh and stepped down from its plinth. He lifted up the quilt to slide into the bed, and when she looked back again he was

164

lying covered over, propped against the pillows, fingers linked behind his head.

'It's not your thanks I want,' he said in a low, angry voice.

She rose swiftly and went across to the window again, her heart thumping, terribly afraid that he might even now spring from the bed to come with his demanding kisses and fierce hard body. 'They seem to be still looking for the boy,' she said, pretending not to have understood the implication of his words. Two of the farmer's sons had come strolling back across the sward, ropes still in their hands, and they stopped and looked about aimlessly as if at a loss to know where to search next. Everybody else had dispersed, and a stillness had descended.

'Come to bed.' He flung out one arm to pat the pillow on the far side of the bed, but she did not see that, and because her nerves were strained to breaking point she raised clenched fists to her temples, and answered him in a harsh scream.

'NO!'

There was silence in the room. Not a sound except her own hard breathing. She knew then that she had severed the last tenacious thread with which he had sought to hold her. He would never approach her again. There was a rustle as he turned over in the bed, and nothing more. Very slowly she let her fists drop to her sides, her fingers uncurling, and when finally she dared to turn her head and look towards him he was so buried in the pillow that she assumed he slept. Only then did she move, making her way across to the door. She slid back the bolt, and went out into the cool white-sky night. There she sat down on the top step, resting her forehead against the old worn post, and did not try to check the tears that ran down her face, and dropped on to her hands.

It was a rustle in the turf roof that stretched down over the gallery that made her lift her head. It was too heavy a scrabbling about for a mouse or an owl. A cat perhaps. Then there was a slithering, and a little grunt. It was the boy!

She could not see him from where she was. Silently she slipped off her shoes, ran barefoot down the steps, and then over the grass for a little way until she could view the roof with ease. There he clung, curled up in the foetal position, wedged on the ledge that jutted out over the gallery with a sheer drop of sixteen feet or more to the ground. She saw at once that he must have clambered on to the rail of the gallery, and then used the deeply notched pattern on the headpost for a foothold to make the final swing over on to the ledge.

Back up again she went until she was directly under him on the gallery. Then she sat on the rail, clung firmly to the post, and leaned out to speak very softly in Dutch. 'Hallo, boy. I saw you earlier this evening, and you ran away from me. I didn't mean to frighten you—only to be friendly. It is very hard to be among people who don't talk our language. They think us strange because we don't speak their tongue, and often they think if they shout at us we must surely realize what they want us to do. We may shake our heads, and even cry a little, but they don't know that we are sad because we are so far from home, and those we love have gone away.'

She paused. The boy did not move, but she knew he was listening intently.

'Someone I love very much disappeared one day, and because I was hurt and upset I did not know what to do or which way to turn. I might have thrown chairs about if I'd been strong enough, or smashed windows, or broken plates, but being a girl I just cried. I still cry often, but nobody else knows. You see, they would not understand. But you understand, and so I can tell you. My name is Jacintha. What is yours, boy?'

There was no reply. But she waited. Then she caught the whisper. 'Claes.'

'That's a good Dutch name. I like that. Claes. Why don't you come down here and talk to me on the gallery? Everyone else has gone to bed.' Then, encouraged by his previous response, she raised herself up, balancing precariously, and met his wide wary eyes. Dangerously she risked putting up a hand. 'I'll help you.'

It was a mistake. He scrabbled out of reach, thin knees slipping, and his pinched little face became wildly hostile. She lowered herself back on to the rail, and started all over again. She talked without ceasing, explaining that sometimes there was a good reason why a father had to leave his son behind at a place where he thought he would be fed and taken care of. 'You see, if he's very poor and cannot get work, it is terrible for him to see his son hungry. That's how your father felt, Claes. He didn't want to leave you—he cried too, but there was no other way for him. At least you know he is alive and well, and one day you'll find him again, but my parents are both dead. Your mother is dead. Did she come from South Holland as I do, Claes? Do I speak like her? My mother used to tell me wonderful stories when I was little. My favourite one was about the dragon who lived in the cave of gold. Do you remember that one? Once upon a time—'

She talked until her throat was dry, but still she went on. Gradually he eased himself down the roof again a little at a time, especially as tiredness made her voice lose strength and he wanted to catch what she had to say. She soon realized this, and lowered it even more, so at last he was peeping over at her, and her hands itched to snatch at him, but she dared not. Her own position was so precarious that the two of them would plunge together to the ground far below.

She lost count of time. The early sun rose, spilling its rays through the trees, and across the still sleeping farmstead. Claes was tired too, his lids kept drooping, and only his slipping when he completely relaxed roused him with a jerk as when a sleeper flails about to avoid falling in a dream, and wakes again. Soon she could catch him unawares. She had untied her neckerchief as she talked, ripped strips from her petticoat hems, keeping the same quiet tone of her voice the whole time, and gradually she had knotted together a band which she hoped would prove strong enough when the moment for testing it came. Now she was talking against time too, for as soon as the farm stirred and he was spotted there would be shouts and running with ladders, and quite apart from losing confidence in her, which she was certain had been built up, he would be likely to panic and fall to his death in the ensuing confusion.

'So I think it will be a good thing for you to leave this place today,' she said, slipping the band around the post, and tying it securely about her waist. 'You'll enjoy riding on Axel's horse. It's a rich deep brown—like the gingerbread men that they sell in the markets at home. You shall have a gingerbread man when you get to Axel's house,' she promised wildly. 'How many buttons would you like him to have? Show me on your fingers. Lean over a little more. That's it. Now let me count if it's five. Number one is your thumb—'

She lunged at him, throwing herself back to pull him to safety with her, and felt the band snap even as Axel caught the boy from her, and whirled him onto the gallery. She went crashing down on to the boards, and although he had tried to break her fall at the same time, he did not stop to lift her up, but rushed the boy into the guestroom.

Her head was reeling with tiredness, and she had caught herself such a crack on the knee that she was almost sick as she tried to move it. But gradually she managed to haul herself up on to her feet, and supporting herself against the wall she almost rolled along it to the doorway. There she stayed, looking in at Axel, who was holding Claes in his arms, talking to him in Dutch in much the same vein as she had been doing. He was fully dressed, and must have been up all night as she had been, waiting intently just out of sight for that moment when he could give her the assistance that she needed, not daring to interrupt. The child, too tired to comprehend exactly what was happening, was already nodding off to sleep. Axel rose, laid him on the bed, and covered him with the quilt. Then he came across to her.

'You had better get some rest as well.' He helped her to the bed. She did not know if he covered her up too. She fell asleep instantly.

It was early evening again when she awoke. There was no sign of Axel or the boy. People must have been in and out while she slept, for there was fresh water in the ewer, and clean towels. A jug of milk and a cup stood on the chest, and she drank thirstily. Then, when she had washed, combed her hair, and put on again the bodice and skirt that had been neatly folded on a chair, she went down the steps from the gallery where she had spent those long hours such a little time before, aware that she was aching in every limb.

The family were only too eager to tell her that Axel had left the farm while the boy was still too tired and sleepy to know what was afoot, thinking to get him away immediately, and was taking him to the couple that she knew about.

'When will he return for me?' she asked in her halting Swedish.

'Tomorrow,' they told her. 'Escort will come tomorrow.'

She was not sorry to rest, for her left hip, thigh and shoulder were painfully bruised, and one knee was swollen, and that night she slept solidly again.

But it was not Axel who came back for her. He sent the Palatine escort that she had had on other occasions, and it was with him that she returned to Stockholm. She knew that she would not be seeing Axel again. In future he would be avoiding her.

There was a letter from him waiting at Reyndert's house for her.. He apologized for urgent government matters preventing his escorting her home again. Claes had shown every sign of adapting to his new surroundings without undue tension and conflict. The warden's wife had made the child the promised gingerbread.

CHAPTER NINE

'I want Lysbeth,' Reyndert announced heavily one evening when he and Jurriaen were drinking together alone in the library. 'There's too many dancing after her petticoats, and it's only a matter of time before somebody tumbles her. And I want her a virgin.'

Shifting his weight, and lounging back in his chair with long-limbed ease, hands cupped about his pewter tankard, Jurriaen regarded Reyndert with an odd, speculative gaze. 'Legally, I trust?' he questioned laconically.

'Of course!'

'I'll remind you of your advice to me that I should select only a suitor willing to show his gratitude.'

'Don't fence with me, Jurriaen!' Reyndert barked irritably. 'You knew then that I was

172

warning you off letting anyone else have her!'

Jurriaen's elbows were resting on the arms of the chair, and he swung one hand towards Reyndert, rubbing thumb and fingers together in a blatant, mercenary gesture. 'How much?'

Reyndert frowned, drained his own tankard noisily, and then wiped his wet lips with the back of his hand in a way that indicated he was preparing himself for a spate of hard bargaining. 'What's her price?'

'Full control of the *Wasa*.'

'What?' Reyndert had almost shot out of his seat, and he crashed the empty tankard down on a side table. 'You're mad!'

Jurriaen's face hardened. 'Are you questioning my ability—or my ambition?' he demanded coldly.

'There's no reason why you shouldn't be ambitious,' Reyndert blustered evasively, 'but you know perfectly well that such an appointment wouldn't be mine to make, even if it were free. That would lie in the hands of Admiral Fleming, and he'll not oust Jacobsson and de Groot now for any reason under the sun.'

'But if they did go,' Jurriaen persisted stubbornly, 'I'd be next in charge.'

Reyndert threw up his hands in exasperation, and slapped them down again on his stout knees. 'How on earth do you think I could ensure that for you?'

Jurriaen's eyes narrowed. 'Suppose I told you that I'd spotted something about the *Wasa* that neither Jacobsson nor de Groot have seen in all these weeks they've been in charge of the building of her? You'd know where to place that information to bring them to disgrace, and myself into favour. Wouldn't you?'

Comprehension dawned in Reyndert's eyes. 'You've discovered an error in Hendrick Hybertsson's original table of dimensions!'

'Hybertsson is dead. The responsibility for the *Wasa*'s sea-worthiness has shifted to those content to go on building her to that sert drawn up by the late Master,' Jurriaen answered, his eyes not denying his companion's supposition.

Reyndert ran his tongue along his lower lip, his expression avid. 'What have you found out?'

Jurriaen shook his head slightly, and wagged a finger. 'Not so fast. My information must be sent direct to the King himself.'

'The King!' Reyndert echoed. 'But he isn't even in Sweden at the moment—'

'Precisely. If I wrote it's doubtful whether my letter would ever come into his hands, and—if it did—he could dismiss it as being too absurd for serious consideration. After all, my name means nothing to him.' There was a slight pause, and then Jurriaen continued with crescent emphasis. 'But if *you* sent him the facts—well, that would be a different matter. At the same time you could recommend my foresightedness in saving the *Wasa* from going down in the first storm that strikes her! Thus can you give me control in the final months of the building of her!'

Reyndert stared at him for a full minute. Jurriaen waited, a smile on his lips, self-assured, confident, well satisfied with the effect of his words. Then, to his astonishment, Reyndert threw back his head as laughter, deep, full, belly-shaking, burst from him. The man's face went crimson with it, and such was its grip upon him that twice he doubled over, giving a glancing slap to his thigh each time as though some other outlet for his mirth must be found beyond the raucous sounds coming from his throat. After enduring this display for as long as his temper would allow him, Jurriaen sprang to his feet, and gripped the edges of Reyndert's coat, hauling him half out of the chair, and then thrusting him back again.

'At least tell me the reason for this insane hilarity?' he roared.

Reyndert choked down his laughter, and gave Jurriaen a placating push. 'Sit down, man. It's a wry joke, and you'll not appreciate it, but it struck me as the funniest thing I'd heard for years.' He rested his elbows on his knees as he leaned forward, his eyes still amused. 'You couldn't lodge such an accusation against the late Hybertsson with the King, and neither would Jacobsson and de Groot have the ship taken from them. You see'—and here Reyndert did allow himself a suppressed chuckle—'the King himself designed the *Wasa*! Hybertsson only drew up the table of dimensions to His Majesty's own instructions!'

Jurriaen sank back into the chair, but gripped the arms of it with sinewy hands, his chin deep in his ruff. 'I didn't know,' he said at last.

'I'm not surprised.' Reyndert had refilled both tankards from a flagon, and he shoved a brimming one under Jurriaen's nose. 'Come on. Drink up. You must direct your highflown aims towards other ships yet to be built. Can you tell me briefly what's the matter with the *Wasa*?'

Jurriaen sighed, and tilted his head back to half empty the tankard in long, thirst-quenching gulps before he lowered it again. Then he compressed his lips ruefully before he spoke. 'There's no reason to keep my observations to myself any more. In a word—unless very carefully ballasted, and I cannot see that there will be room enough in the bilge—she'll prove top heavy. Her superstructure is far too bulky and heavy for so narrow a hull and sharp bottom. I'll point all this out as tactfully as possible to Jacobsson tomorrow—I don't suppose de Groot would give ear to any criticism of his late brother's work. After all, Hybertsson must have thought the King right, or he would never have gone ahead with drawing up the ship in such a way.'

'I know those who would pay you to continue to keep silent on the matter,' Reyndert said quietly. The atmosphere in the room became tense, almost palpable, and slowly Jurriaen raised his glance from the ale he had been absently swilling round to meet Reyndert's cunning eye.

'Who?' Jurriaen asked bluntly.

'Sweden's enemies.'

A slight smile touched Jurriaen's mouth. 'So you have a variety of contacts! I suspected it, but I wasn't sure.'

'Shall I put you in touch?'

'Wait a moment. You're not a man to do this out of generosity. It's obviously going to result in our mutual benefit—but how?'

'Naturally my thoughtfulness in putting this suggestion to you will not go unrewarded by those concerned, and you'll be able to demand far more gold for keeping your silence than would have made payment of your wages had you been the master shipbuilder from the time the keel was laid!' He showed his gap-teeth. 'In return for helping you to twist fortune to your advantage, I want Lysbeth.'

Jurriaen's smile broadened unpleasantly. 'For the *Wasa* I would have taken her by the scruff of the neck, and thrown her to you, but things are very different now. To be frank, I don't think you stand a chance, and I'll not force her,

177

but'—here he gestured expressively—'if you can win her affections you may have her by all means.'

He lifted his tankard, held it out to his companion, and drank. Reyndert, disappointed and surly, followed his example more slowly.

*　　*　　*

'Jurriaen is late,' Lysbeth said uneasily, glancing towards the clock. He had failed to come home in time for the supper and revels that Reyndert had arranged for the entertainment of some visiting Dutch officers. Lysbeth had enjoyed herself, for several of the gentlemen had been young, lusty, and personable; she had flirted gaily with them all, and allowed one fair and dashing youth such kisses and caresses in the garden that he had sworn to desert his ship and stay to be her adoring swain. He had not meant it, and she had not believed him, but it had been a highly enjoyable interlude for both of them, and distracted her mind from Jurriaen's absence.

But now everyone had gone. Reyndert had escorted his guests back to their ship, and the servants were clearing away glasses and sweetmeat dishes, and setting the furniture back into place. It was not that Jurriaen did not often go out without a word as to his whereabouts; in fact, much of his mode of living was similar to that which he had followed in Amsterdam where he had been forever out on affairs of his own of which they knew nothing. Yet he usually made a point to attend all the functions held in Reyndert's house, and only the evening before had announced his pleasure at the chance of meeting one of the officers again as they had known each other during childhood. Yet he had gone out quite early before she had gone upstairs to change, and had not returned.

'Come to bed,' Jacintha persuaded from the foot of the stairs, her hand on the newel post. 'Jurriaen leads his own life, and he'll not welcome any inquisitive concern, as you know well enough. No doubt he's gaming somewhere, and found the tables too great a pull to break away.'

'I suppose so,' Lysbeth answered, picking up her taffeta skirts as she followed Jacintha up the stairs. She would have lingered on if it had not been for the chance of Reyndert returning before Jurriaen, and she had no wish to find herself alone with him. She had become expert at evading that situation, but in such a way that she was certain that he did not see through her little ruses. She had caught several heavy looks from him that evening, as though her gaiety with the officers had roused him to strong desire, but she had turned aside his jealousy with sweet and secret smiles, making much play with the ivory fan that he had given her, implying that he could set his mind at rest.

Jurriaen still had not come home when she was ready for bed. The shutting of the entrance doors, which had sent her darting to peep over the bannisters down into the hall, had only announced Reyndert's return. She had drawn back quickly, afraid that he might glance up and see her, but he had gone across into the salon where all the candles were still alight. Back in her own room, she had finished undressing, slipped a robe over her nightshift, and snatched up her tortoise-shell hairbrush before going along to Jacintha's bedchamber as she often did to talk over the events of the evening.

'Reyndert is home,' Lysbeth said, clambering up on to the end of Jacintha's bed to sit with her back resting against the carved post as she brushed her hair for the allotted length of time that she felt was needed daily to keep its gloss and softness. 'He was quite boorish after supper, claiming two dances that I had intended for someone else.'

Jacintha, sitting back against the pillows looked sternly at her sister, and wished it wasn't ever her task to reprove, warn, and admonish. It made her feel old and staid and prudish, which she was not. Circumstances had dampened down her light-heartedness, her natural impulsiveness, and her longing to abandon herself uncompromisingly to love, but beneath her composed exterior these aspects of her character merely lay dormant, checked by self-discipline, as well as the overwhelming sense of responsibility that she had always had towards Lysbeth, and which had been given an added impetus by their father's death and all that had followed.

'Reyndert is infatuated with you, and I think your conduct is most unseemly. I begged you not to accept those trinkets he has been buying for you. He thinks you're giddy and empty-headed enough to be bought with such gew-gaws.'

'Then he's wrong, isn't he?' Lysbeth replied airily. 'I did try to be strong about not accepting after that lecture you gave me, but he seems to find such pretty things. I cannot resist them.'

'You're impossible!'

Lysbeth shrugged a vague protest. 'I like him well enough as an acquaintance, and he must surely understand that there can never be anything more. It's not as though he were some inexperienced boy—indeed, he was married once, and his wife died in childbirth soon after they came to Sweden.' She grimaced delicately. 'His breath is foul, his belly fat, and the palms of his hands ever red and sticky with sweat. It's not my fault if his conceit is so great that he thinks I see any charm in him.'

'You've encouraged him, Lysbeth,' Jacintha

exclaimed severely, 'and you cannot deny it. From that first evening we arrived you started to play the coquette, begging instruction on the spinet, asking him countless questions, and hanging on his answers in a way that few men could resist.'

Lysbeth grinned at her triumphantly through a veil of hair caught by the brush's bristles. 'I saw he was much taken with me already, and decided to use it to my advantage. It was obvious that he was a man of some consequence in Stockholm, and could open doors for us that might otherwise remain closed. I had made up my mind to enjoy myself here in Sweden. Jurriaen did little enough entertaining in Amsterdam, always bent on outside pleasures that did not include us, and I found the company at the Pieterzoons excessively dull, even though it did give us the chance to exercise our French sometimes.' The bristles released her hair, and she shook it back from her face, her expression hard and self-satisfied. 'And has it not proved to be a sound investment of but a little time and trouble? Reyndert has been content for us to stay on here—and indeed I truly dreaded being landed in some outlying country cottage such as abound in the precincts of some of the shipyards. You have also found it most convenient for these social duties that you have taken upon yourself.' Then she leaned forward, resting her weight on the flat of one hand plumped deep in the bedcovers, and added in a burst of confidence: 'Moreover, Jurriaen soon let me know that he approved of my encouragement of Reyndert. Jurriaen and I are very much alike—we care for comfortable living, and money to spend carelessly—and Reyndert has introduced him to many people who can further his career very profitably.'

Jacintha stared at her incredulously. 'You are allowing yourself to be used to suit Jurriaen's purposes just as cold-bloodedly as you have been twisting Reyndert around your little finger for your own ends!'

Lysbeth gave her a long, quiet look that was almost pitying. 'There are many ways of serving the man one loves, Jacintha. And all the time there is no other woman of consequence in Jurriaen's life. I live in hope that one day he will at last turn to me.' Then she set to brushing her hair more vigorously, and it crackled into tiny sparks.

Jacintha watched her sister with grave, unhappy eyes. But what would happen if Jurriaen ever turned against Lysbeth, and disillusioned her with some act or word that would destroy that blind, unquestioning, immature adulation? Lysbeth was still more child than woman, but the day must come when she would see him as the weakling that he was. And Jacintha prayed in her heart that when it came she would be there to sustain Lysbeth when everything shattered about her.

'It would be wise to move from this house,' Jacintha said after a few moments. 'I'll bring the subject up again with Jurriaen, but until now he has always refused to discuss the matter, saying that it suits him here.'

'Then I don't suppose he'll change his mind for your reiterated opinion,' Lysbeth remarked, wholly unconcerned.

Jacintha lifted a hand in a gesture of appeal. 'I beg you to return all that Reyndert has given you, and to take nothing more!'

Lysbeth smiled as she tossed aside the brush, and shuffled foward on her knees to put her hands on Jacintha's shoulders. 'You worry about me too much,' she said, resting her cheek briefly and affectionately against her sister's before drawing back again. 'You always have done, you know. But I can look after myself now.' Then she slid from the bed, bidding her goodnight, and went from the room, her robe trailing ribbons behind her.

But Lysbeth did not sleep for quite a little while. She stood at the window until she saw Jurriaen come riding home at such a spanking pace that she thought he must be thinking that he could catch the tail-end of the festivities, and have a word with his old acquaintance. She blew him a kiss from her fingertips which he did not see as he tossed the reins to a servant that ran out from the stables, and flung himself into the house. Then she took off her robe, and slipped into bed. She was soon asleep.

Downstairs Jurriaen was pacing up and down in the salon, his face congested with an almost spluttering rage. Reyndert, who sat solidly in a red leather chair, followed his movements to and fro with eyes as sharply alert as though watching a tennis ball being knocked over a net.

'They refused to give me any further payments! Said what they'd already given me was enough for my silence!' Jurriaen thundered.

'It was a generous sum, you must admit,' Reyndert said coolly.

'But that was to be the beginning!' Jurriaen hurled himself about, and thudded his clenched fist down on the table. He spoke through his clenched teeth. 'I'll go down to Jacobsson tomorrow! The ship can be righted! A longer bowsprit, and careful ballasting! They'll not make a fool of me!'

'If you do that,' Reyndert said carefully, 'I'll be forced to reveal that I suspected your dealings with enemy agents, and had you twice followed to your rendezvous. I chose reliable men who will not be disbelieved in a court of treason.'

Jurriaen's face screwed up in disbelief at what he had heard. 'What are you saying? You're as deeply involved as I am!'

'It's not the first time I've routed out

unsavoury characters for the Swedish government,' Reyndert continued as though Jurriaen had not spoken. 'The humble folk who come to these shores are not my concern—it's the intelligent and the cunning who have to be watched. In my unique position of liaison I have the opportunity to spot those who come to spy, and others who are also not to be trusted.'

'But you led me into this mess!' Jurriaen protested. 'I had not thought of telling anyone except the King himself!'

'Nobody will believe you.'

Incredulous comprehension thundered home in Jurriaen's brain. 'You were paid more than I! Those devilish Poles—'

'That is my affair,' Reyndert said impassively.

'I will tell the truth!'

Reyndert held up his hand. 'I must warn you of what happened to four shipwrights who committed a much lesser crime than yours. They refused to work until they were paid what they said was owing to them, and were condemned to death for mutiny. They had to run the gauntlet six times between two hundred and sixty men, who beat them to a pulp.'

'Oh, merciful God!' Jurriaen put a shaking hand over his eyes as though to blot out the scene he had envisaged.

'Now let that be an end to your ranting and raving, for it's all to no purpose.' Reyndert lifted his foot, and kicked a chair forward. 'Sit down now. Have a drink, and be thankful that you've made some profit from this little venture. Moreover if the *Wasa* does go down in a storm—and nobody but you seems to consider such a possibility—no blame will be laid at your door.'

Jurriaen collapsed into the chair, set his elbows on his knees, and dropped his head into his hands. 'What madness allowed me to be influenced by you?' he groaned with desolate bitterness.

'I'm very glad you were. Lysbeth is proving difficult to snare. You can assist me. I shall sweeten the bait, and you must close the trap. That's my price for keeping silent about a crime that could see you garrotted on the yard-arm of the *Wasa* itself!'

CHAPTER TEN

It was only afternoon, but already the days were shortening as Jacintha saw the two orphans on to the Dutch ship at Dalarö that was to take them back to their grandparents' care. On deck she thanked the sea-captain for the help he had given her. He was a brawny man with a severe facial expression, but a kindly look in his long narrow eyes.

187

'I have money for the seaman who has volunteered to take the children from Amsterdam to Haarlem,' she said, taking some coins from her purse, but these were promptly waved aside.

'One of my officers is to deliver the children when he goes home to his wife and his own little ones in that town. Put your money away and your mind at rest, Juffrouw. All is well.'

She stood on the quay to wave to the children, and watched the great canvas sails unfurl amid a whirlpool of screeching gulls. The ship drew away, leaving a pale wake on the choppy sea. A great wave of homesickness swept over her, so violent, and so painful, that her heart seemed to contract with it, and she knew that if it had not been for Lysbeth she would have taken a passage on that vessel herself, and left Sweden and all ties with Jurriaen behind her for ever.

Her short return journey to Stockholm was in a hired carriage with a number of passengers from a newly-arrived ship, all Swedes returning to their own country, and their pleasure at being home again, the delight with which they viewed the scenery passing by, seemed to increase the pain of her own homesickness, which she could not shake off.

When she alighed near the Castle walls she decided that a little exercise would be welcome after the cramped and bumpy ride, and instead of turning towards Reyndert's house she walked along by the water's edge, and came at last to a grassy mound, which she climbed slowly. The wind was bitter with the promise of the first snows of winter, stinging her face, but she welcomed its buffeting vigour as though it must surely lift her heavy mood, and she made no effort to control the swirling of her tawny cloak and skirts. At the top she could see across to where the *Wasa* lay, black against its grey setting of wharf and water. It had been instrumental in bringing her to Sweden, but she felt no animosity towards it. In a strange kind of way it fascinated her, as if in some indefinable way she and the vessel were linked on some mutual course of destiny.

The wind was getting stronger, and Jacintha drew her cloak about her as she retraced her steps. Leaves and rubbish went whirling about her feet, and the branches of the trees were in wild disorder. She feared that the Dutch ship had run into a storm.

The way back to Reyndert's residence seemed long, and the way was ill-lit. Her heart began to pound, and she quickened her pace almost to a run, desperately afraid, and yet not knowing what she feared. It was with an almost absurd sensation of enervating relief that she saw the large house loom into sight behind its walls of imported Dutch stone.

The house was wonderfully quiet and still

after the restless night outside, and she shut the door behind her, leaning against it for a few moments as she regained her breath, and mocked herself for her irrational fears. Yet then it came to her that the deep dread lying in the pit of her stomach had not lessened. She had thought that it had been the wind that had caught her up in its unknown terrors, but it was some other danger, as yet unknown, that filled the air all around her.

Then there came from upstairs a scream so terrible that her blood was chilled. 'Lysbeth!' she gasped, and grabbing up her trailing skirts she flung herself up the stairs, and along the passage to hurl the door open into their apartments.

A strangely motionless scene met her eyes. Jurriaen stood by the settle as though he had just sprung to his feet, and his hands were hanging at his sides as he looked down at Lysbeth, who was curled up in a twist of her blue velvet skirts, her arms clutched about one of his high bucket-booted legs, her head against his thigh.

'What is it?' Jacintha demanded of Jurriaen. 'Why did Lysbeth scream?'

Jurriaen raised his head, and there was fear and uncertainty in his face. 'I've just told Lysbeth that Reyndert has asked me formally for her hand, and I've agreed that she shall marry him.'

Lysbeth whimpered, and clutched him all the tighter when he would have pulled away. 'Oh, Jurriaen! I beg you!'

'You cannot force her to such a marriage!' Jacintha cried angrily. 'He repels her!'

'That has not been my impression of their relationship,' Jurriaen blustered. 'It has pleased her to accept the gifts he's lavished upon her.'

'She's young and foolish and greedy! Let Reyndert have back all the trifles he has given her!'

'Black pearl ear-drops are not trifles, Jacintha. No young woman could accept such an offering except as open encouragement to the man concerned.'

Jacintha drew in her breath. 'I've not seen such ear-drops!'

Jurriaen leaned down, took Lysbeth's face by the chin, and jerked her about. Her eyes were shut, the tears streaming down under the lashes, and from her ears hung the exquisite pearls.

'Lysbeth!' Jacintha exlaimed in dismay. 'Take them off!'

'It's too late!' Jurriaen said determinedly, and tried to prevent Lysbeth as she tore at her ears, her sobbing abandoned and noisy, and hurled the ear-drops away. He stepped back when she would have clawed at him again. 'Get up! Compose yourself. Anyone would think I hadn't chosen a husband who'll give you

191

everything you can wish for—this fine house, clothes, jewellery, and an established position in a society that you've made no secret of enjoying!'

'But she does not love him!' Jacintha stormed in protest.

Jurriaen's eyes narrowed with desperate impatience. 'Lysbeth will be well settled for the rest of her life. There is no-one who would not approve of this arrangement that I've made for my ward. Since when has it been customary for young girls to raise their voices against those in authority over them? They do as their fathers—or their guardians—bid them. I cannot believe that Lysbeth's affections towards Reyndert can wax and wane within the hour.'

'I love no one but you, Jurriaen,' Lysbeth moaned, bowed over in her wretchedness.

'Then seek to please me, or I shall be forced to send you back to Amsterdam!'

'No!' Again Lysbeth screamed, and hammered her fists upon the floor. But Jacintha darted forward, dropping to one knee beside her sister, putting one arm about her shoulders, and looked up at Jurriaen in appeal.

'Let us go back home! We'll ask nothing of you ever again! Our grandfather's allowance is enough to keep us from poverty. You can be rid of us!'

Jurriaen was enraged that Jacintha had taken up his idle threat. 'That would suit you very well, Jacintha, but that was not what I had in mind!' he elaborated wildly to subdue her. 'I should arrange that Lysbeth be cared for in an orphanage until such time that I saw fit to take her under my roof again. She could return home in custody with those who are deported for criminal offences from time to time. You would stay here!' He made a downward prodding movement with his forefinger.

'I'd not let you separate us!' Jacintha rose to her feet again, and faced him doggedly.

'You'd have no choice!'

'Jurriaen, Jurriaen! please, please!' Lysbeth was reiterating a childish, blubbering appeal over and over again, lying face downwards, her head within the hollow of her arms. He looked down at her with angry disgust, and prodded her with the toe of his boot.

'God's wounds! Get up, and stop your snivelling. Reyndert is not a brutal man, and he'll use you kindly enough. You have a little time before he returns in which to make yourself presentable. Find those ear-drops and put them back on—they'll soften up your feelings towards him again.' His tone became sly and wheedling. 'I happen to know that he's chosen a ring and a necklace to match. Think of that! You can get anything you like out of him if you make some show of amiability when he seeks to pleasure you.'

Lysbeth's head came up with a jerk, and she

half-raised herself on one elbow as her forearm went up to sweep the tangled mane of her hair from her eyes. Her upturned, tear-blotched face, the lids red and swollen, the mouth loose and trembling, was distorted by the aversion he had roused in her. In stunned stupefaction she stared at him for several moments as though he were crumbling before her eyes.

'Send me home, Jurriaen! Far, far, far away from—you!'

He struck her a savage blow with his fist that made her scream out as she was hurled backwards across the floor.

*   *   *

Catherine looked at Jacintha with compassion. 'There is nothing I can do. Your guardian has every right to arrange a suitable match for his ward, and you must understand that your being in Sweden can make no difference to his authority over you and your sister. Have you talked to Master Leeghwater?'

Jacintha nodded. She had begged him not to pursue his demands for Lysbeth's hand, but he was adamant. 'I'll be a good husband to her, Jacintha,' he had said, his set face showing that he was not to be swayed. 'That fool Jurriaen must have bungled everything. She was sweet enough to me when I gave her the ear-drops, and if only she would let me talk to her, instead

194

of staying shut up in her room and refusing to eat, I would soon bring her round again. God knows what he said to turn her against me like that!' His mouth was ugly, denoting a combined anger against both Jurriaen and Lysbeth. Then when Jacintha had pointed out again that Lysbeth did not love him, he raised cynical eyebrows. 'Love? What has that to do with marriage? When Lysbeth has plenty of babies to keep her busy she'll give no more thought to such romantic nonsense. I'll look after her, and she'll lack for nothing. But the marriage contract has been drawn up, and the sooner Lysbeth accepts the fact that I intend to wed her the better it will be.'

'Why are you so against Master Leeghwater?' Catherine asked. She felt sympathy towards Jacintha for her concern for her young and headstrong sister, but it was not as if the girl's heart was already set on someone else. Even then Catherine would not have considered it a viable reason for turning down an excellent marriage offer. Everyone knew that young girls could become infatuated with the most unsuitable men and cherish dreams of living in bliss that took no account of anything beyond a handsome face and a dashing appearance. She herself remembered falling deeply in love with a young officer with whom she would have gone to the ends of the earth, but a fine scoundrel he had turned out to be, and she had thanked God many times for her father's intervention in what could have been a disastrous affair. No, it was better to take no heed of displays of temper and wild threats of suicide, which simply gave excitement and drama to a situation, and when the time came for her own daughters to wed she would see to it that they were guided firmly in the right matrimonial direction, however much they might seek to find other more rosy-looking arbours for themselves.

'I fear he will be cruel to her, Madame. There is no gentleness in the man. I cannot trust his word.'

'His word?' Catherine echoed, and she smiled at Jacintha. 'I hardly think Master Leeghwater would hold the position he does if he could not be relied upon as a man of honour by both his own government and ours.' She shook her head kindly. 'You are so young yourself, and little experienced yet in being able to judge others. My advice to you is to let matters ride for a little while, and give your sister time to adjust to the idea of this marriage, and point out gently all the advantages in it for her.'

'There is no time left, Madame,' Jacintha said dully, all hope gone that in some way the Countess would be able to intervene. It was not that Lysbeth had not become resigned to the marriage, for after the first wild bouts of hysteria a terrible lethargy had settled upon her, and she became wholly compliant, showing neither interest nor distress at the preparations for the wedding that were going ahead. But Jacintha's fears had grown. Even Jurriaen was afraid of Reyndert now, but for what reason she could not suppose. Greatest of all was her terror that Lysbeth's apathy was merely a prelude to a final self-violence.

Outside the Palace Jacintha did not retrace her steps back to Reyndert's house, but turned in another direction, her hands tucked in her fur muff, her breath hanging before her in a cloud. Winter had settled in, making the days black, and the city was ice-locked. Her enquiry at some ground floor apartments of a house in the market square sent her hurrying off again, and when she reached the *Wasa* a workman went at her bidding to take a message on board.

Axel appeared at the head of the gangway, and came down towards her, one gloved hand on the rope that formed a rail, his head slightly down against the swirling snow, his black cloak billowing. Under the wide flat brim of his high-crowned hat his eyes were set on her face. He stepped on to the wharf, and stood in silence, waiting for her to speak.

'Axel,' she said unsteadily. 'I do not love you, and cannot pretend to any change of heart. But I'm asking you to marry me.'

CHAPTER ELEVEN

Lysbeth looked round as Jacintha in cloak and hood entered the bedchamber, dragging with her one of the iron-bound chests that had brought their belongings from the Netherlands. 'What are you doing?'

'Packing,' Jacintha answered, throwing the lid up, revealing that her own things had almost filled it, and then going across to the closet. 'We're leaving here. Get everything out of the chest-of-drawers, and your shoes, and boots. Take nothing that has ever been given you in this house. Your betrothment is at an end.'

Slowly Lysbeth rose to her feet, her expression stupefied. 'Is it true?' she whispered with a little fending gesture of her hand as if to keep at bay the tremendous force of her relief that would come should this miracle prove to be as Jacintha had said.

'True enough.' Jacintha's speech was abrupt and emphatic, matching her movements as she took one garment after another out of the closet, folded them, and packed them down. There could be no doubt. Lysbeth gave a low cry of joy, and rushed to throw her arms about her sister burying her face against her neck, tears running, no words coming, but only by the pressure of her embrace could she convey

198

her feelings at this moment. Jacintha, after one swift, speechless hug in return, put her firmly from her.

'Get the other chest out for me, and do as I say. The sooner we get away from here the better.'

Something in her tone made Lysbeth's first wild happiness subside. 'What is it? Has Reyndert not changed his mind? What has happened?'

'I cannot explain now. Just make haste.'

Lysbeth, in a kind of terror that some minute of a delay would send her whirling back into that black abyss from which she had just been rescued, flew about the room as she gathered up her possessions, throwing them without neatness or order into one chest and then the other, leaving Jacintha to put them to rights. Finally when everything was packed and the lids closed, Lysbeth put on her cloak and hat. Jacintha glanced about to make sure nothing of importance had been overlooked.

'The servants can bring these boxes down for us. Now we'll go.' She took a firm hold of Lysbeth's hand, and led her from the room. Downstairs in the hall they heard the sound of angry voices in the salon. Jacintha straightened her shoulders, lifted her chin, and flung the door open.

'We are ready to leave, Axel,' she said. And her husband of one hour turned about to come towards her.

'Wait a minute!' Reyndert roared, and pushed Jurriaen aside as he thrust his way around the table to come over to her. 'You're not taking Lysbeth out of this house! She's betrothed to me, and Jurriaen is still her guardian!'

'No longer,' Jacintha answered. 'It was laid down in the agreement that was signed in Amsterdam on the night that Lysbeth and I first arrived in Jurriaen's house, that in the event of my marriage before hers all responsibility for her well-being should revert to me. There is nothing that you or anyone else can do now to stop her coming with me.'

'You've forgotten one point!' Jurriaen shouted savagely, fear of what the consequences of this turn of events might mean to his own safety in the light of Reyndert's vengeance had taken all his colour from him. 'I did not give my permission for you to marry Captain Halvarsen! I'll have it annulled!'

Axel, who was standing at Jacintha's side, put his arm protectively about her shoulders. There was a glimmer of satisfaction in his eyes. 'If we were in the Netherlands you would have some power behind your threat, but we have been married by Swedish law and God's blessing has been laid upon our union. Nothing can untie that knot! Come, Jacintha.'

The servants had carried out the chests and

set them in the large horse-drawn sleigh that was waiting outside. Lysbeth, who had overheard the whole discourse from a nervous distance, flew in advance of Axel and Jacintha to clamber into the sleigh, and hurl herself into the farthest corner, afraid that even now Reyndert might try to snatch her back by sheer physical force. But he knew better than to tangle with a man of Axel's standing. Already he feared the social and political consequences of this embarrassing scene, and regretted bitterly his display of temper. A word against him in the ear of Count Palatine could get him sent back to the Netherlands. There was one thing he could do that might stabilize the situation apart from a carefully worded apology for his outburst. He turned to Jurriaen, and spoke incisively, the effort of controlling a desire to give vent physically to his wrath making his face blotched and patchy.

'You are going to be on the next ship back to Amsterdam, Haaring! Hand in your resignation to Jacobsson and de Groot, expressing your regret at not being able to continue work on the *Wasa*, or—by God!—you shall face trial for your recent treachery to the Swedish Crown before the week is out!'

Jurriaen gave him a look of black, unremitting hatred. Then he strode out of the room and up the stairs to throw his own belongings together, and get out of the house at once. There was a vessel leaving for the Netherlands again tomorrow, and he knew he must sail with her. His time in Sweden had come to an ignominious end, but Reyndert Leeghwater had not heard the last of him. There was a way in which he could take his revenge, and from a very safe distance.

Axel drove swiftly to the house in the market square where Jacintha had enquired after his whereabouts only that afternoon, but it was a bitter night, and the sisters were thankful to be greeted by a crackling log fire that filled the hearth, the flames leaping up the chimney, and went to warm themselves, holding out their numbed fingers to the blaze. Jacintha had seen at once that her new surroundings were essentially the small compact residence of a busy man needing a city *pied-à-terre*, which although furnished and hung with tapestries that reflected his sophisticated and stringent taste was obviously not regarded by him as a home.

Lysbeth, feeling less chilled, turned about to glance at everything. 'There's not room for me to live here,' she declared judiciously. 'We'd be falling over each other.'

Axel, who was removing a stopper from a flagon set with some glasses on a side table, glanced across at her. 'Just for tonight, Lysbeth. Tomorrow we must make some other arrangements. I have an idea that we can discuss later.' Then he poured wine for the three of them, and it was Lysbeth who gave the toast, although the jerkiness of her speech showed that she had little faith in the conventional words she offered, having no illusions as to why Jacintha had entered so swiftly into this marriage of convenience. 'I wish you both great joy in all the years that lie ahead.'

Conversation over supper was stilted and spasmodic. Lysbeth, her first exultation in freedom over, was at first very subdued and unnaturally quiet, but then Axel made the suggestion that she might like to join the ladies in the Palatine entourage, and her spirits rose high. She glimpsed again a life of social pleasures as though a door had opened for her, throwing sunlight into her face.

She talked about it later as she and Jacintha shared a large recessed bed. 'They say that when King Gustavus Adolphus comes home for the winter from campaign there is no end to the feasting and jollity, and the Queen is transformed. German musicians come to court, and there is orchestral music and evenings of dancing, masques, and every kind of merriment. The King is very handsome, I've heard, and much accomplished on the lute—he often plays for the company. Oh, think of it, Jacintha!' She clapped her hands together, her elbows resting on the coverlet, gazing ceilingwards where the firelight was making flickering patterns. Already the past was fading from her mind.

Jacintha listened without comment, and was only glad that with the resilience of youth Lysbeth was recovering both from the shock of Jurriaen's betrayal, and the misery of the last few weeks. To her own future she could give no thought. Tomorrow she would be alone with Axel for the first time as his wife, and must share his bed.

In the night she awoke with a start, crying out, 'Constantijn!' Outside the snow was falling steadily.

'Now I'm going to take you home to Halvarsensgaard, Jacintha,' Axel said next morning. He had just returned from taking Lysbeth to the Castle. Catherine had received the new member of her household graciously, and then handed her over to those of her ladies who were to take the girl under their joint wing.

Axel helped Jacintha into the sleigh, tucked furs around both of them, and then with a flick of the whip they slid away across the square. Once free of the city he urged the four black horses to a tremendous pace, which sent the long tails swishing like the plumes of a fan, and glittering crystals of hard snow went flying up from the thundering hooves.

It was an exhilarating ride through a landscape that was blue and silver and white, sliced through by the tall trunks of the forests, and the foaming sapphire of plunging rivers half choked by ice. There was an accompanying jingle of bells and harness, and the arrow hiss of runners. Sometimes Axel gave a shout when he had to stretch almost flat, his feet against the dashboard, as he pulled hard to check a great sweep down the curve of a way already marked by other, smaller sleighs that had been about earlier that day.

Jacintha, her fur hood drawn tight about her face, her cheeks stung to rose by the fierce air, sensed how Axel glanced at her time and time again, although they spoke little. Once when she did catch his eyes as he turned towards her she surprised a darkly speculative look, which disappeared instantly as he smiled, his breath like spume in the frosty air.

'Fast enough?' he challenged. And with devilment she shook her head. Then the whip cracked and whirled, and the sleigh seemed to lift and fly as the treetrunks flashed past in a hundred shades of grey, black and indigo. He laughed, throwing back his head, and she shouted in her excitement, urging the horses on, her hair streaming out from under her hood, her gloved hands clutching the rail.

'Faster! Faster!' Then she shut her eyes, and felt only the swirling hiss of movement, the bitter wind in her face, and remembered where she was bound. The spark of her mood died away. She relaxed back in the seat again, pulling the furs up to her chin. Gates were looming ahead. They went speeding through, over the virgin snow of a drive which was shown only by the pines lining it, and came to a slithering halt that sent up a white shower like spray.

'Here we are!' Axel jumped out, and servants came running to take the horses' heads. He ploughed through the soft snow to come around the sleigh, put his hands under her armpits, and swung her across the steps of the porch. She looked up, and the great black timbered house seemed waiting to swallow her up.

Inside it was vast with a stairway heavily carved, panelled walls hung with the antlers of elk and reindeer. All the rooms led into each other, and Axel watched her with amusement as she went on a tour of inspection, casting aside muff, gloves, scarf, hood and cloak as she went, her heels tapping on the bare plank floors as she stared with unabashed curiosity up at the brightly painted wooden ceilings with their primitive designs of birds and flowers, and then lowering her gaze to stare at the massive settles, the enormous tables that could seat fifty in comfort, the chests, the vast chairs, and rough benches strewn with the skins of black bears to offer some modicum of comfort on the hard seats.

'This a hall of Vikings,' she remarked with

some awe, and spun about with a swirl of her skirts to view him as she spoke. He was standing squarely in one of the doorways, hands set low on his hips, feet set apart, and seemed to fill the frame with his size.

'Our family's house has stood on this site for two hundred years or more, and there must have been other, more primitive buildings before that. The gardeners have dug up axe-heads and horns and plate.' There was pride in his voice, but slowly it hardened towards her. 'Many brides have come here, but none more reluctantly than you, Jacintha.'

'I was honest with you.' She was quickly on the defensive.

'Honest,' He repeated wryly. 'Oh, yes. But I think I might have been tempted to have traded your honesty for a few sweet lies had the choice been mine to make.' Then he turned away and walked back through the rooms. She heard the barking of dogs that came rushing to greet him.

He drank quite a lot after supper, sitting with one booted foot propped against the square corner chimney, tilting his chair back and swaying as he eyed her steadily over the rim of the tankard that he put frequently to his lips. The firelight played on his face, and flashed ruby lights from his rings. She sat on a stool, her back aginst the wall, opposite him. She was tired, and her lids were heavy, but she would not surrender to her weariness.

'I'll take you to see Claes tomorrow,' he said. 'He's a changed boy—he's put on weight, and apart from occasional bouts of ordinary mischief he doesn't get into trouble any more. The warden and his wife have become very attached to him.'

'I'm glad,' she said.

'You're tired, Jacintha.'

'A little.'

'Why not go to bed?'

'It is very late.' She stood up.

'Do you know the room?' The four legs of the chair thumped back on the floor as he rose too.

'Oh yes,' she said hastily. 'The maidservant showed me where she had unpacked everything.'

Quickly she picked up a thick red wooden candlestick, and the flame streamed flat, making the wax drip in the draught as he opened the door for her. She went across the hall, and mounted the stairs in the little golden aura of light. The boards creaked underfoot as she went along to the massive door that led to the main bedchamber.

Then the floor creaked again behind her, and she knew that he was following her. Perhaps he feared that she might bolt the door against him. But that was not her intention. She left it wide open as she went through. The great carved bed glimmered in the candle light, the linen turned back over a cover of creamy fox fur.

208

CHAPTER TWELVE

It had been snowing again during the night. White crescents rested along each small pane, and the whole room was lighted by its glow. Jacintha closed her eyes again, feigning sleep. Axel's rising from the bed had awakened her, and from under the deep warmth of the covers she had heard him go into the adjoining closet to wash and dress.

He was coming back into the room. His quiet footsteps halted beside the bed, and she knew he was leaning over to where she lay curled up in the middle of it. His fingertips, cool and gentle, brushed back a strand of hair from her forehead, but she did not move. Then the door closed behind him.

She relaxed, and rolled over on her back, lifting one bare arm above her head to rest it on the pillow. There was wonder in her mind. There had been some kind of empathy between them in their coming together that had gone beyond the physical joys and ecstasy to which he had introduced her. If her heart had not been so locked in love for Constantijn, she might well have come to care for this exciting, passionate man. But the old obsession was still with her, and however much she might have wished otherwise, in view of making life so much easier for both herself and Axel, she knew that Constantijn would keep her yearning for him through all the years to come.

She threw back the covers, but it was bitterly cold in the room, and she shivered. Catching the furs about her, she went across to the window, stepping over her scattered garments that lay about the floor. But the panes proved to be so thickly lace-frosted that she could not see out. She glanced over her shoulder and saw the candle that she had just managed to set down last night before he had seized her.

She went across, still dragging her vast robe, and lighted it. Then she took a coin from her purse in a drawer, and with the aid of curling irons she held it in the flame until it was hot. Back she went to the window, and using a handkerchief not to burn her fingers she held it against a pane until a perfect little spy-hole appeared. She put her eye to it, and viewed with delight the sparkling world that stretched as far she could see.

There came a barking just below, and out of her line of vision, but after a few moments an excited, leaping tumble of grey and tawny sledge-dogs appeared with Axel in the midst of them, holding their harnesses high, and pulling a light sledge. He was going off on some outing without her! She could not endure to miss such a trip on so breath-taking a day! She rapped frantically on the glass, but even if the barking had not drowned the tapping he could not have seen her. In exasperation she rushed across to fling open the massive door, went dashing along the passage, and down the wide flight of stairs, her furs enveloping her and flapping behind in a train. The icy air made her gasp as she stepped on to the porch.

'Wait for me!' she cried.

He was crouching down to slip the first harness over the leader's neck and chest, and he glanced towards her with mingled amusement and surprise. 'I had no intention of going without you,' he reassured her. 'I was just getting them ready.'

When he entered the house later she was dressed and had breakfasted, and was fastening her cloak.

'Jacintha.' There was question in his voice as he set his hands on her shoulders. But if he expected her to raise her mouth for a kiss he was to be disappointed, for she pretended to be confused with hooking the clasps, keeping her attention down, her head bent. What had happened the night before had not changed her feelings towards him at all, and she could not pretend a show of affection that was not there.

His hands fell away, and he stepped back. His face had hardened at the deliberate snub. 'I'm taking you to the warden's cottage to see Claes,' he said tonelessy as if the pleasure of the day had already gone for him.

Claes must have seen them coming down the hill. He came bounding out of the cottage to meet them, and it was only when he saw that Axel was not alone, and had a passenger on the sledge, that he came to a halt, drew back, and returned indoors again.

'He's still a very nervous child,' Axel commented.

The warden's wife came out to meet them, bobbing curtsies in her excitement at the visit, and when they entered the cottage there was no sign of the boy. But there had been a scuttling up the ladder to the sleeping-loft. Jacintha called up to him.

'Have you forgotten me already, Claes? I told you all those tales of magic and adventure the night you were on the roof. I've been told that you have grown tall and strong. Let me see if this is true.'

He came then, shyly, reluctantly, but step by step down the ladder, and she saw that he had been well-fed and well-cared for, and he was neatly and warmly dressed in stout peasant clothes and good boots. A little prompting from the warden's wife induced him to make a bow, and his last fears went when Jacintha produced some oranges and sweetmeats for him in a basket that she had held under her cloak. Then he went straight to Axel with some news of his own to impart, still clutching the oranges, and was lifted up. Jacintha saw that there was liking

212

and respect between the two of them, and their talk was of skis that the warden had made for the boy, and of a sledge that Axel had brought on his last visit.

Seeing the child so content, and remembering the terrible conditions in which she and Axel had found him, Jacintha determined that when they returned to Stockholm again she would continue with renewed vigour her efforts to seek out those of her countrymen who were in need of help.

They stayed for several weeks at the country house. Axel taught her to ski and to drive the sledge and the sleigh, and they went skating on the nearby lake. Occasionally he went hunting, but because the law forbade the use of skis for the pursuit of elk that could only flounder in deep snow he went on foot on these expeditions far into the forest, and she was always anxious until he returned, not caring what the bag might be. One night she awakened to hear the most strange and plaintive howling in the distance.

'What's that?' she asked in a whisper, lifting her head from the pillow. Then she raised herself up quickly on one elbow as the eerie sound came again.

'It's only a wolf,' he muttered sleepily, but he became instantly alert as she huddled close to him in the wide bed. It was the first time she had ever drawn near on her own accord, and with a wild rush of hope he scooped her into his arms, believing that at last he was to find the love in her heart that she had withheld so rigorously from him even in moments of deepest passion. But the old disappointment had not been banished. The love that he longed for was still directed towards somebody else.

It was the quiet swish of skis that heralded the end of their stay. A messenger in blue and yellow livery came swooping up to the house, bringing letters of importance for Axel. Jacintha, sewing by the fire, looked up as Axel came into the room. He had broken the seal on one letter and was already reading through it, a deep frown on his face, but he had kept separate another letter, which he handed to her, speaking almost absently. 'One for you, Jacintha.'

'It's from Lysbeth!' she exclaimed happily. It was written in the neat, careful hand that Lysbeth had cultivated long ago, for their father's hasty scrawl, which even made his signature on a painting almost illegible, had always exasperated his younger daughter. Lysbeth was enjoying life enormously, and thought the King the most handsome man she had ever seen with his splendid height and physique, his strong features and pointed golden moustache and beard. There were so many gay events, and she had learnt all the new dances. There seemed to be a new young swain in Lysbeth's life, although to judge from the number of names that sprinkled the letter he was not alone in his pursuit of her. Jacintha folded it up, intending to impart the news of it to Axel, and saw that he had already taken up a quill to pen a reply to his own letter for the waiting messenger to take back to the city.

'We must return to Stockholm tomorrow,' he said, dashing sand on the ink, and then waxing and sealing the letter. 'All is not well with the *Wasa*.'

*　　*　　*

Jacintha found the town apartments very small, but also cosy after the large house that they had left only that morning. They had a quiet supper together in the firelight.

'I must go straight to the *Wasa* tomorrow morning,' Axel said, lighting his long-stemmed pipe as he sat back in his chair. Then he waited until the servant had finished clearing the dishes before he continued. 'A very serious accusation has been made. Your former guardian, Jurriaen Haaring, has written from Amsterdam to both Hein Jacobsson and de Groot to say that unless they lengthen the bowsprit to a full twenty-five feet, and arrange so much ballast in a certain way, the *Wasa* will prove top-heavy in rough weather. He says that he only withheld the information on the insistence of Reyndert

215

Leeghwater, who declared that the King—having decided on the ship's dimensions—would be greatly embarrassed by such an exposure of this error of judgement. But now Jurriaen feels he can no longer remain silent.'

'That sounds a little odd to me,' Jacintha said ruminatively. 'How could the King's embarrassment be weighted against the possible loss of several hundred men and the ship itself?'

'There's more to it than that. Jurriaen delcares that Reyndert made the suggestion to him that foreign agents would pay him to keep silent on the matter. This was so abhorrent to him that he could no longer stay under Reyndert's roof, and returned to the Netherlands at once.'

'Could that be true?' Jacintha asked doubtfully.

'True or not—Leeghwater will find himself and his past affairs being thoroughly investigated. If he has been up to anything he'll certainly live to regret it.'

'Why should Jurriaen feel so certain that something is wrong with the *Wasa* when other, more experienced men have failed to notice anything?'

'He's quite frank about it. One of his ships went down off the Shetlands, and when he made his own private investigation into the cause of it, he realized that its bottom was too narrow, and it had no proper belly—both faults

216

he declares he recognized in the *Wasa*.'

'I'm very glad that Jurriaen has written about it,' she said, 'but it's all very strange.'

The next morning they took a small one-horse sleigh, and drove through the city to Skeppsholmen. Jacintha had intended leaving Axel there and driving on to the Castle to see Lysbeth, but when he put aside the fur-wrap and alighted he saw how keenly she was eyeing the ship, and thought to please her.

'Would you like to come aboard? I can find someone to show you over it while I'm in conference with the shipbuilders.'

'Oh, yes!' Jacintha answered eagerly, and was quick to get out of the sleigh. While Axel took the reins, and saw that the horse was securely tethered, Jacintha ran her gaze over the ship again. So much progress had been made since she had last viewed it close at hand! The steep narrow lines of the completed sterncastle rose so high as to make the ship appear almost scoop-shaped, both rows of gun ports had raised covers ornamented with lion masks, and a large sculptural group had been placed into position forward around the forecastle and the beak head. Busy as ants a score of men were shovelling new fallen snow off the top decks and hurling it over the sides, but a white crest of it rested crown-like on the leaping leonine figurehead that extended far out above the blunt, bulging bow, and from the snarling

217

mouth icicles hung thickly like frozen saliva.

Standing on deck amidships Jacintha stared upwards at the soaring masts, and felt dwarfed by the great size of the ship. One of de Groot's young assistants was asked to conduct her over it, and seemed much pleased by the duty assigned to him. He pointed out various points of interest, and then took her below. Everywhere men were hammering and banging, and there was a strong smell of paint. Most of the activity was going on by the light of lanthorns, for although the dark winter's day outside received some radiance from the snow it was a different matter inside the ship where except for the fitful illumination it would have been black as night. Only where the windows were glazed in the stern was it easier to view the splendid inboard carvings. Through the door that opened into the Captain's cabin, where already Axel and some other gentlemen had gathered, Jacintha glimpsed the exquisitely carved panelling and moulding, and was invited in to look around at close quarters before the meeting began. But it was by the light of the lanthorn swinging in her guide's hand along a gallery that Jacintha caught sight of the mermaid.

'Wait a moment, please,' she said, slowing her pace. 'This one interests me very much.'

Her guide was surprised. They had viewed so many of the fantastic sculptures that embellished the ship, and by comparison this little caryatid, which was very similar to those forming roof decoration outboard on the port side lower gallery, deserved little more than a passing glance. But he held the lanthorn high, and its pale glow illumined carved features that somehow looked strangely familiar to him, and he was deeply puzzled. There was the high brow, the straight nose with the sweet curve of nostril, the finely moulded lips, and determined little chin, that somehow he knew. From under the sloping crown, set with carved jewels, which had already been painted in reds and greens and gold leaf, the yellow hair fell in thick, heavy waves down to the bare breasts with the softly raised roseate nipples.

Then as he glanced towards Jacintha he saw in that instant that she and the mermaid were the one and same. 'By heaven! Did you model for Master Tijsen?'

She smiled, shaking her head, and touched with her fingertips the mermaid's hips to where the gold-leafed overlapping scales carried down over the twisting tail. 'I visited his workshop once, and spent some little time there. He has paid me a very pretty compliment. I'm certain that he did it unconsciously, merely bearing a suitable face in his mind's eye, but it is very flattering for me—and exciting—to know that my likeness is on this splendid ship. I must bring my husband to see it.'

But Axel did not see it that day. He was already back on deck, standing by the foremast on the forecastle, taking part in a fiery discussion with the two shipwrights and some other gentlemen, which involved a great deal of gesticulating towards the bowsprit, when Jacintha came up again after the tour that had taken her all over the ship from the cannon-ball store to the bricked galley where the great cooking-pots had already been installed. She waited impatiently to catch his attention, but it was not until the whole party had streamed down on to the wharf to make observations from that angle that some decision appeared to be reached. Then Axel, looking around for her, found her waiting a few yards away.

'Did you enjoy seeing over the ship?' he asked, taking her by the elbow and swinging her with him towards the sleigh.

'Oh, yes!' she exclaimed, hurrying along with him, 'and there's a mermaid caryatid that looks just like me. Could we not go back on board just for you to see it?'

'Not now,' he answered, his thoughts so steeped in contemplation of what had been decided that he scarcely heard her. 'I'll leave you at the Castle, and then I must see Admiral Fleming. They cannot see that there is any fault with the ship's dimensions, but they're going to extend the bowsprit to almost thirty feet.'

She did remind him about the caryatid later

on, and he fully intended to seek it out, but every time he went on board it was on some official business, and the matter slipped from his mind. But then winter had receded, and the breaking ice, holding golden sun-crystals in the depths of its bobbing chunks, allowed the *Wasa* to be moved to a mooring by the gun-crane near the palace where it made a graceful sight on water that had captured the acid-blue of the clear spring sky. And Axel, called upon to give his attention to other affairs, left the *Wasa* in the hands of those in charge of getting her ballast of stones aboard and stowed away.

Jacintha was thankful to see the sun's return. The bitter weather had caused much hardship amongst the poorer Dutch families, particularly when a prolonged blizzard of exceptional force brought work to a halt in the shipyards, and wages—never promptly paid—became long overdue. She had gone daily to visit those in trouble, had seen that the sick received care, fought for the disabled to receive some compensation, and done her best to keep away near-starvation with food donated by those of her countrymen more well-to-do.

Lysbeth, unabashed by the past, shrugging off all responsibility for the marriage to which Jacintha had committed herself, had continued on her gay and selfish way. But then a stalwart young Swedish sea-officer, whose name was Hans Odenburg, and to whom she had been growing more deeply attached, departed on a short voyage to fetch some of the armament for the *Wasa* from a gun foundry a little farther north. So greatly did Lysbeth miss him that when his ship returned she showed that he need no longer have any doubt about her love for him. He came to see Jacintha, and she guessed at once the reason for his visit. She had come to know him quite well, for he had been Lysbeth's escort at all the most recent social gatherings, but it was the first time she had ever seen any nervousness on his healthy, rugged features, and he ran a hand over his straight, dark-streaked fair hair, cleared his throat unnecessarily, and coughed several times.

'I wish for Lysbeth's hand in marriage,' he said at last. When this was granted by Jacintha, who felt only relief that her sister had fallen in love with such a respected and well-liked man, he pressed his request still further in a desperate, pent-up burst of words as though he feared refusal. 'Would you allow us to wed soon? I love Lysbeth dearly, and long to have some time ashore with her before I sail with the *Wasa*.' Then not giving Jacintha time to answer he continued with argument. 'The war is spreading again now the winter is over, and General Wallenstein is already marching towards the Baltic shores—'

'You have my permission to wed as soon as Lysbeth wishes it, Hans,' Jacintha interrupted him, and smiled at his efforts to control his ebullience. He shot out of his chair, bowed, kissed her hand, her cheek, and crossed in two swift strides to open the door into the hall where Lysbeth, whose presence Jacintha had suspected, was waiting. They embraced ardently, and then returned to Jacintha, laughing and happy, and their talk was wholly of the future. It was only when they were leaving again that Hans remembered another matter that he had promised to bring to Jacintha's attention.

'Last week Admiral Fleming held some capsizing tests on the *Wasa*. Thirty men ran from one side of the ship to the other, and on the third run she keeled over so sharply that a couple of men fell into the icy water. Both were rescued, but one caught a chill, and has the sweating sickness. I was told that you would visit him.'

'I'll go now,' Jacintha said, and went to fetch her cloak. She had become used to such summons, and although she always tried to be home whenever Axel returned there was nothing to make her return in haste that day as he had gone south to view some defences.

The address that Hans had given her took her to one of a dozen small cottages that stood on the outskirts of Skeppsgaarden. It was no great distance, but she took the little mare that Axel had given her, a sweet-natured rust-coloured animal with a mane and tail pale as tow. An old peasant woman, hired to cook and clean for the workers who lived there, came with a key to unlock the door.

'I'm glad you've come, my lady. I've not time to sit by a sickbed half the day.' She swung the door open, and left Jacintha to enter the dark little cottage alone. The patient lay in one of the narrow wallbeds.

Jacintha slipped off her cloak as she went across to take the hand that lay on the coverlet, and look down into the flushed, feverish face that turned towards her. It was Constantijn.

CHAPTER THIRTEEN

In the driving seat of the little cart borrowed from one of the master carvers, her mare between the shafts, Jacintha drove at speed out of the city. Behind her Constantijn with his head on a pillow lay wrapped in blankets and smothered in furs. He was too ill to care about anything, and had no idea where he was being taken. All that he was able to comprehend was that in some miraculous way Jacintha had come back to him, and he kept calling out her name just to make her answer, fearful that she might have disappeared in one of those strange swirling dreams that seemed to make him weightless and send his head floating about in the oddest way. Each time she answered him, and her hand came down to touch his face in reassurance, and then he slept again.

The forests on the way to Halvarsensgaard were full of pink and white windflowers, and everywhere the snow had gone except in deep crevices in the rocks higher up the hillsides. The way was steamy in parts where the forest was seeping out of the ground to meet the sun, but although there was a great deal of mud the mare kept up a spanking pace, enabling them to cover the distance in good time.

As no word of warning of arrival had been sent ahead, she found the gates of the house closed, but she jumped out and thrust them wide, and then drove up to the porch. The servants came from all directions as she flew into the entrance hall, issuing orders.

'Wrap hot bricks for the bed! Light all the fires! I need extra blankets—some light broth—everything for a poultice!'

She ran ahead up the stairs, past the carved door that led to the room that she had shared with Axel, and into the next one where she rushed across to pull open the inner shutter, and let in the light.

She watched three of the manservants settle him in the bed, and another went to set blazing the dry birch logs that were always stacked ready for lighting in the hearth. The wisdom of bringing Constantijn here under this particular roof, although Axel himself was far away, had not yet crossed her mind. All she had known was that neither the cottage that he had shared with other workers nor the small town house had been suitable places for the nursing of a man in the grip of a severe sickness that only care and warmth, and long nursing could overcome. Here at Halvarsensgaard there were sensible, level-headed country maidservants, whose help would be invaluable.

'Jacintha!' He was calling her again, unable to see her from the depths of the soft pillows and heaped covers, struggling to sit up. She flew to him, motioning the servants to leave, and sat on the bed, snatching up his hand in hers, and pressing it lovingly against her cheek.

'I'm here, dear love!'

He shook his head slightly in bafflement. 'I wrote to you. Is that why you came? Why didn't you answer?'

'I never received any letters. Jurriaen had moved to a new address. I searched for you every day in Amsterdam.'

He closed his eyes, frowning as he tried to sort out the facts in his mind, the effort almost defeating him. 'I was made to serve on a corn-vessel going north. Jumped ship at Dalarö. Tramped to Stockholm, and got work on the *Wasa*.'

She leaned over him, her voice eager. 'Could

226

it have been you who carved the mermaid?'

He smiled, his lids flickering open, his gaze meeting hers. 'You saw it?'

She nodded, her mouth tremulous. 'But I had no idea that it could be your work. I must have missed seeing you a dozen times. Oh, Constantijn! To think that we should meet again like this!'

Then a knock on the door made her start up, and the women came in with the broth, hot bricks, and everything else she had ordered. She was aware of their curious glances, but gave no sign of it, and she slipped into the role of nurse, competent and reliable, which she had played so often before for others.

His fever soared during the night, and she was kept busy attending to him. He no longer knew her, and flailed and threshed about, but she found capable and intelligent aid as she had expected in the assistance of Maria, a maidservant no longer young, and together they kept him sponged down, and as cool as possible. He shouted and laughed, and rambled on unintelligibly, but when morning came he made no sound, and the fever was still rising.

Jacintha glanced up and met Maria's dubious gaze on the other side of the bed. 'He's not going to die!' she said through her teeth. 'I will not let him die, Maria!' She ripped back the covers. 'Get more cool water and hand me that sponge!'

227

It was evening again when at last the fever broke. Jacintha, who had not slept or rested, sank to the floor on her knees and spread out her elbows on the bed, dropping her forehead on to the back of her hands. Her hair was tangled, caught back with a ribbon that had slipped free, her dress soiled, and her sleeves ragged where she had torn off the cuffs when they had got in the way. Maria put a respectful hand on her shoulder.

'Go and rest, Madame. He will be all right now. I'll set Helga and Solveig to watch over him.'

Obediently, like a child, Jacintha rose, and went with dragging feet along to her own room. There she flung herself across the great bed, her cheek buried in the soft furs, and slept.

*　　*　　*

At first it was easy enough to turn aside the questions that Constantijn asked. He was so weak, and so quickly tired that he slept for much of the time, but then the day came when the brief explanation of how she came to be in Sweden was not enough, and he demanded outright to know where he was, who owned the house, and why she was in it.

'Have you no idea, Constantijn?' she asked quietly, looking across to where he lay propped against the pillows, his eyes hollow, his face sharp and thin. She was sitting in a high-backed chair by the window, unaware that the sun's rays had made a bright aura of her hair, the glow following the line of cheek and chin.

'I think you are married, Jacintha,' he said soberly, 'and this is your home.'

Her gaze did not falter. 'How did you know that? I have not worn my rings.'

'You have such authority here. The servants run at your bidding. Where is your husband?'

'He has been travelling up the coast, but will soon be returning to Stockholm. In a few days I must leave here, and be there to meet him. Maria will look after you, and you must get well and strong. Stay as long as you like—we shall not be using the house until the summer. Lysbeth is shortly to be married, and I must see to the arrangements for her wedding.'

'Do you love him? Your husband?'

She rose abruptly, and turned away from him as if she could not bear his searching eyes upon her face. 'No,' she said tonelessly. She was still a stranger to the man whose life she shared. The love that she cherished was of the heart. Tender. Yearning. Of such sweetness that just being near Constantijn made her want to weep with happiness, and the thought of parting from him again was so terrible a burden that she felt weighed down physically by it.

'Why did you marry him?' he asked bitterly.

She moved restlessly, clasping and

unclasping her hands. 'I had no choice. It was the only way I could regain authority over Lysbeth at a time when she was desperately in need of help. Had I known that you were in Stockholm I would not have gone to Axel.' She spun around, her voice fiercely accusing in her anguish. 'Did you not hear Jurriaen's name? Did you not think who he might be? Could you not have searched for me as I did for you?'

He looked distressed. 'I heard him mentioned, but such an ordinary name among so many others. I believed you to be still in the care of some elderly guardian far away in Amsterdam, whose trade or profession I did not know.'

She nodded with a sigh, and her hands fell listlessly at her sides. 'That is true, Constantijn. Forgive me for my outburst.'

'Come here.' He held out his arms to her, and without hesitation she ran across to lie on the bed beside him, closing her eyes in joy as he kissed her, and enfolded her in his arms. She buried her face against his neck and clung to him as he whispered softly to her. 'Dearest Jacintha. I love you—I've never stopped loving you. Do not go back to Stockholm. Stay with me. Another few days, I'll be back on my feet, and then we'll leave here together. Ill fortune parted us, but now we have been given a second chance, and we must take it.'

She felt a wild surge of hope. Was it possible?

Could they really stay together after all? 'But how? Tell me!'

'We could get a ship at Dalarö, and go home, Jacintha! Think of that! Together!'

'Home!' she echoed, and felt drunk with the wonder of it.

'I'd get work easily enough in Amsterdam now—Master Tijsen would give me credentials.'

Then doubt returned to depress her mood, and she drew away from his arms to look down into his face. 'How shall I tell Axel? He knows that I do not love him, but I'm his wife, and he has been good and kind to me.'

'Are you going to let someone else part us again?' he demanded incredulously, seizing her wrists. Colour flushed patchily into his cheeks, and he began to cough in his agitation. Quickly she soothed him down.

'Hush! We've talked enough for today. Sleep a little while, my dearest.'

He relaxed, but kept hold of her, and she did not move, although the sun went down and the light faded. She watched him all the time. If only words of love had not been exchanged between them again she could have borne the parting, but not now. The strength and determination that had sustained her through difficulties in the past had melted away, leaving her as enervated and helpless as if a great tide was sweeping her out of her depth, and she had

231

neither the will nor the desire to swing against it.

The days went past, and Constantijn proved to be a difficult patient, querulous and moody. It irked him to be under the roof of the man whose authority he feared, knowing how easily Jacintha could be taken from him, and he became subject to black moods of depression, which hindered his convalescence, and he would be flushed and feverish again, railing at his own weakness, and making it a hard task to quieten him.

The strain told on Jacintha, and taxed her until she felt as severely confined by the walls of the sickroom as the patient himself. Then one afternoon when Constantijn was sleeping she looked out of the window at the countryside bursting with the spring that seemed to come overnight in all its glory in this strange Northern clime, and felt an overwhelming desire to walk for just a little while in the clean sweet air.

She summoned Maria to the sickroom. 'Sit with the patient until I get back, Maria. I'm going for a walk.'

'It will do you good, Madame. Don't hurry. I'll not move from the bedside.'

She ran with almost wild relief through the woods, unable to constrain her delight in being out of doors. The lilies-of-the-valley had raised their white blooms everywhere, and after a while she slowed down to a walk, pausing in one glade and then another to pick a large bunch of them. She clasped the long stems in both hands, inhaling the fragrance of the flowers as she wandered along.

She walked far, and was away from the house much longer than she had intended. But she felt revived and refreshed both mentally and physically as she turned for home, quickening her pace, eager to see Constantijn, and to take up her duties again.

She ran upstairs, and threw open the door of the sickroom, holding the nosegay high. 'Here I am! Look! I've brought you Spring itself—' Her voice trailed off as she stared in disbelieving horror around the deserted room. The bed was empty! Made up with clean linen and smoothed quilt as if Constantijn had never been there. All the decoctions of syrup and herbs that she had prepared for his cough had vanished from their place on a side-table. Of his bed-robe and slippers there was no sign.

'Maria!' she screamed, dropping the lilies-of-the-valley in a sweet-scented shower as she flung about to go tearing back downstairs to find out what had happened. Then she halted with a gasp. Axel stood squarely in the doorway, barring her way. His expression was very calm and restrained, and unable to comprehend his mood she was more frightened by it than she would have been by a contortion of rage.

'Where is he?' she demanded hysterically.

'Not in this house.'

'You've sent him away!'

'That is correct.'

'Did you make him crawl then?' Her voice was frantic. 'He could not walk!' She would have dashed past Axel, but he caught her by the arm, and swung her back into the room, bringing the door closed to behind him.

'Do you think me so lacking in Christian charity that I would treat a sick man in such an inhuman manner?' he asked sternly.

She refused to be comforted, throwing her clasped hands over her bowed head as she swayed in her anguish. 'He's still so ill! He could die if he had a relapse!'

'He'll not die.'

'Let me go to him, I beg you!'

'Not yet.' His words with their hint of promise made her drop her hands and raise her head hopefully, but he did not elaborate at once, and strolled across to the window. There he stood looking out as if lost in contemplation of the view.

'When?' she implored, losing patience. 'I love him, Axel. It was he whom I would have married if ill chance had not torn us apart. Do not keep me from him now!'

'He said something of the same to me. I understand that you wish to return to the

Netherlands together.'

'Yes.' She whispered it. There was a long pause before he spoke again.

'I make one request of you, Jacintha. Stay with me until the *Wasa* sails. I'm going with her as military observer for the King.'

'When will that be?' she asked warily, fearing a trap and yet unable to see where it could lie.

'Early in August.'

'Then you will release me.'

'I give my solemn oath on it.'

She was nonplussed, but she knew she could trust him. 'I suppose that means that I must not see Constantijn again until then.'

He turned and looked at her. 'I would deem that an honour to be so considered,' he said gravely and with dignity.

She understood. He bore a proud name and did not want it sullied by scandal. When he sailed she could depart unnoticed to the Netherlands, and by the time he returned the gossiping whispers and speculation would have died down. The least she could do was to save him painful embarrassment.

'Very well. May I write to Constantijn?' she asked anxiously.

'Only to explain the agreement that we have reached, and later to make all the arrangements for your voyage home together that must be after the *Wasa* has sailed. More than that I cannot condone.'

She nodded. It had all been so much easier than she had anticipated, and the enforced separation of such a comparatively short time after so much waiting without hope would not be too hard to bear. But she would have to phrase the letter with utmost tact.

'May I write at once?'

'The letter shall be conveyed without delay.'

She went straight to the cupboard where pen and ink were kept, and he left her alone as she wrote a long and loving letter. In it she reassured Constantijn that her marriage with Axel was at an end, and the last few weeks were to be a hollow sham to keep up appearances. She signed and sealed it, and gave it to Axel.

He tapped a corner of it against the palm of his hand. 'Constantijn is at the warden's cottage. Maria is there to nurse him. You need have no fears that he will not recover.'

She pressed the back of her hand against her mouth to keep back a sob as she turned away. 'Thank you for telling me. I'll not break my promise not to see him.'

'I know that,' he said evenly, and went to send the letter on its way.

They left for Stockholm an hour later. She saw the cottage in the distance as they drove by, and watched it until a clump of trees hid it from her sight.

But her marriage was not at the end that she had supposed it to be. That night Axel made love to her more ardently than ever before. And she understood. He intended that she should be pregnant when the time came for her to leave him.

CHAPTER FOURTEEN

Jacintha packed Axel's wooden sea-chest. It was the last small duty that she could perform for him, and she wanted to add the pocket sundial she had bought him, and a pewter stoop that she had given him one natal day. She did not know why she sought to put some reminder of herself amongst his effects, unless it was to show her gratitude for all that was past. They were parting amicably, and she was still at a loss to understand how a man of such violent passions could treat the situation in such a quiet way. It was not that he was not torn by it. She saw the strain in the throbbing of a nerve in his temples, the tautness of skin over bone, and the shadowed look in his eyes. His gaze followed her continually, and when she turned her head by chance and caught his look it was deep enough to drown in.

She folded his winter cloak, and put it in last of all. There was no telling how long the *Wasa* would be at sea, or what battles she would fight. War clouds were regathering ominously, and the new man-o'-war was a powerful striking force. Closing the lid, she snapped the clasp, and turned the key. As she rose to her feet she saw that Axel had entered the room, and he stood watching her. He looked very fine in his buff jerkin with the orange sash, the falling ruff of multi-pleated lace, long narrow breeches, and soft bucket-topped boots. In his hand he carried his wide-brimmed black hat with its gold cabled band. 'It is ready?' he asked.

She nodded, and he motioned to two seamen waiting in the hall, who came in to lift it up, and carry it away and down to the ship for him. Then he came forward, and took her chin in his hand, his eyes searching her face as if imprinting her visage on his mind for ever.

'Will you not change your mind and come with the *Wasa* as far as Vaxholm? There all the visitors are to be put ashore,' he said.

He wanted to prolong their parting, and that she would not do. The ship was going to be full of people, and it would be better to part here in private instead of waving from a crowded shore-going dinghy.

She shook her head slowly. 'That would not be wise,' she said. Her heart was beating painfully, and she had not realized how agonizing this farewell would prove to be.

'Have you nothing to tell me?' he asked, a desperate throb of appeal in his voice.

She lowered her lashes. She knew what he

meant, but could not bring herself to tell him what he wanted to hear. 'You have been a good husband to me,' she whispered huskily. 'I'll never forget you. God go with you on this voyage and keep you ever in His grace.'

He kissed her then. A long loving kiss. Without rancour. Without reproach. Only with love. Then he swung about and left her. She heard the door slam, and his footsteps hurry away down the street. She sank down into a chair, her whole body shaking, and sat for a long time with her fingertips pressed over her eyes. Somehow not being able to cry made their parting all the more poignant.

Then at last she stirred and made ready for her own journey, putting a grey cloak over her yellow gown, but moving in a heavy, almost lethargic way. All her belongings were packed ready to be slung on to the hired horses that Constantijn would bring for the short journey to Dalarö where they would go aboard a Dutch ship for Amsterdam.

She wished that Lysbeth could have come to see her off, but her sister would be on board the *Wasa*, sharing the last minutes with her bridegroom of just a few weeks. In any case Lysbeth had received the news of her leaving with Constantijn with stony hostility. 'You are a fool, Jacintha!' she had said. As on some other occasion that now evaded Jacintha's memory.

She was thankful when Constantijn arrived,

excited to see her again, his kisses eager, his embraces almost boisterous, full of talk of how he had missed her, the voyage that lay ahead of them, and how glad he would be to get away from this stony-faced country and back to the Netherlands again. All this took place on the doorstep where she had been waiting for him, and he suddenly glanced beyond her into the house.

'Has he gone?' he asked sharply.

'An hour ago.'

He nodded, and turned about to bring forward the horse that she was to ride. He helped her into the side-saddle, and she sat watching him as he picked up her baggage and strapped it on. When all was ready he swung himself up on to the horse beside her, and gave her a wide smile. 'Now we're really homeward bound, Jacintha.'

They moved off along the street, which was busy with people going towards the quay at Lodgaarden just below the Castle of the Three Crowns where the *Wasa* lay. If their way had not taken them also in that direction Jacintha still would have wanted to see the ship once more, and even Constantijn, who had been on board only the day before fixing a piece of his own work, a door lintel with tritons holding a shield with the Royal crown above the captain's quarters, was as eager as she for a last glimpse of the warship.

It came into sight, and they reigned in together to gaze at it. Encrusted with magnificent sculptures, all vividly painted, ablaze with gold leaf, its double row of scarlet lion-headed gun port covers open to reveal the polished bronze cannon muzzles, and with an added brilliance from the glazed windows of the galleries beneath the great coat-of-arms of the Royal house of Vasa topping the stern, the *Wasa* shone like a ship of jewels on the still water. Everywhere people had gathered to watch her leave, and it seemed to Jacintha that most of the city's ten thousand inhabitants must be present. Some were already cheering and waving, and the visitors on board were crowding the rails, and waving back.

'It will be a sad day when she goes down to the bottom of the ocean,' Constantijn said gravely, leaning forward on the saddle-bow.

Jacintha shivered superstitiously. 'Do not speak of such a misfortune!'

Constantijn's expression did not change. 'It will go down the first time it meets rough weather.'

There was no doubting the conviction in his voice. Jacintha turned to look at him in apprehensive puzzlement. 'How can you be so sure?'

He flicked a resting hand from the wrist expressively. 'You forget that I was one of the men that took part in the capsizing test that was carried out. Believe me, that ship nearly went down that day! Thirty of us had run together from one side to the other. The first time it went over by the breadth of one plank, the second by two, and the third time three—and that was when I and another fellow fell in. Then the testing was stopped!'

'Probably it was not properly ballasted then,' she argued faintly.

'Perhaps not.' He shook his head sagely. 'But I wouldn't sail on that ship, and neither would anyone else in his right mind who had seen the test that day.'

She looked back at the *Wasa*. Axel had seen that stability test just before he had gone south to view the defences. She remembered how the ship's master, Joran Matsson, had come to see him the following day, and they had been deep in a private conversation that she had not disturbed. Only when Matsson was leaving did she inadvertently overhear a snatch of their talk. Matsson had just reached out for his hat, and jammed it solidly on his head. There was a heavy note in his voice. 'You've done everything in your power, Captain Halvarsen, and so have I. God grant that we're both to be proved wrong in our judgement, and the others right after all.'

At the time it had seemed a strange remark, but it had meant nothing to her, and as Axel had not chosen to discuss the matter she did not

242

question him. But now its meaning was only too clear. Both men had been convinced that the *Wasa* would not stay on an even keel. When Axel had left her today he was certain that he was going to join a doomed ship, and would not return. That was why he had raised no objection to her leaving Sweden with Constantijn. All he had asked of her had been these last few weeks spent with him, and during that time he had hoped that a son would be conceived, so that some part of himself remained with her, and for the future. And she had not told him!

'Constantijn,' she said in a low tense voice. 'I cannot go with you.'

'What?' He jerked about in the saddle, making the horse move restlessly, and stared at her with mingled astonishment and consternation.

'I must speak with Axel.'

She would have moved forward, but he reached out swiftly and seized the reins. 'There's nothing you can do to stop him sailing with her! He cannot opt out of his official assignment!'

'I know that,' she answered, 'but there's something I must tell him.'

He was displeased, his expression showing disgruntled resignation as he acquiesced. 'Very well. We'll ride down to the quay, and I'll wait for you.'

Her face was curiously sorrowful as she gazed at him. 'I shall join the visitors on board, and sail as far as Vaxholm.'

His eyes narrowed, and he shook his head slightly as if he disbelieved his own hearing. 'But that means we would miss our ship to Amsterdam!'

'What you have just told me about the *Wasa* has made me realize that I must stay in Sweden. There can never be any return to the Netherlands for me. You must go alone.'

He went very pale, and his lips became tight and thin. 'But this is what we've been waiting for all these weeks! To be together! To go back home as if all this time between had never been!'

'It's no use,' she answered with a low, determined note in her voice. 'We cannot pretend that those weeks have not existed. I'm going to have a child.'

From an immediate reaction of shock his features moved to become dark and congested with a bitter jealousy, and his hand shot out to grip her arm so fiercely that she uttered a cry. His voice was harsh. 'But you wrote—!'

'I didn't know when I sent that letter to the warden's cottage that Axel wanted a son!'

'Did you intend to let me think it was mine?' He was outraged and incredulous.

She tried to screw her arm out of his grasp, her face sober and withdrawn, her eyes unrepentant. 'I wanted the child loved—not rejected in any way.'

'You cheating little—'

'Do not dare!' she cried witheringly, and tore herself free. She whirled the horse about, but he dug in his heels and brought his own mount sharply forward to block her path.

'Jacintha! Wait! Forgive me! I'll father the child, and treat it as my own! Sail as far as Vaxholm if you must, but come back to me! We'll let the Amsterdam ship go, and take another!'

'I cannot, Constantijn.' There was a strange blending of compassion and desolation and triumph in her voice, which was beyond his comprehension. Then she leaned forward, touched his face with quivering fingertips, and then resolutely moved her horse away, and went off at a canter towards the ship. He did not follow her.

CHAPTER FIFTEEN

Such a crowd had congested near the ship itself that she had difficulty in getting through, and people turned startled and annoyed as her horse came moving between them. But from her vantage point above their heads she saw that the boats that were to warp the *Wasa* along past

Skeppsbron were already in position, and there was every sign that departure was imminent. In desperation she slid from the saddle, and darted on foot between the clusters of spectators and was finally forced to elbow her way through the crush. 'Let me pass, I beg you! A thousand pardons, but I must reach the ship!'

She broke from the crowd at last, and stepped on to the gangway just as it was about to be drawn away. She gave no one any time to say whether or not she should still go aboard, but plunged up it in a dishevelled flutter of ribbons and disarrayed cloak. Eager hands helped her on to the deck, and she was thrust through until she stood in the centre of the maindeck. Breathless and agitated she looked around for Axel.

The ship was crowded. It seemed to her that there must be five hundred or so on board. Quite apart from the ship's crew, which numbered well over a hundred in itself, there was a company of soldiers, the wives and families of both the military and sea-faring men, and a host of elegantly dressed dignitaries, and their ladies. Jacintha moved amongst them, straining her neck to look for Axel's tall head, but there were so many large men, and a dazzling confusion of silken cloaks and clouds of hat plumes, which made it difficult to view at any distance.

A great cheer went up. The *Wasa* was

moving! Gently she was being edged out from her berth by the small boats just ahead of her, and below on the upper battery deck the capstan was turning, deep voices raised in a cheerful shanty as the men wound in the heavy hawser anchor. All around on shore the cheer went echoing on, taken up by a multitude of voices that made it rise and fall, and resound again. Vespers were over, and the congregations had streamed out of the churches in the soft evening sun, adding their numbers to those that already made up a multi-coloured spectacle of their own as they waved neckerchiefs and kerchiefs in every hue. All around the *Wasa* a flotilla of rowing-boats and other small craft was gathering to act as an impromptu escort, their small flags bright but limp in the quiet air.

'Have you seen Captain Halvarsen? Is my husband up there near the stern-post?' Jacintha questioned those whom she knew and many that were strangers to her, but although some had seen and spoken with him none knew where he was now. Then suddenly she heard her sister's voice exclaim in astonishment close at hand.

'Jacintha! What on earth are you doing here?' Lysbeth, vividly clad in gown and be-plumed hat of coral velvet, had broken away from a group near the mainmast, and was coming towards her.

'I'm looking for Axel,' Jacintha explained

247

desperately. 'Have you see him?'

Lysbeth gave her a curious look. 'No—but then the ship is so crowded.'

'Where is Hans? He might know!'

'You cannot ask him yet,' Lysbeth answered with mingled pride and regret. 'He's on duty.' And she indicated with a little nod of her head the spot where her slender young husband, proudly sashed in crimson silk, which had been her own handsewn gift to him, stood by the more portly figure of the *Wasa*'s Captain Söfring Hansson, who was directing operations with barked orders through his speaking trumpet. Then she added in a happy conspiratorial whisper, ever wrapped up in her own affairs with little thought for others: 'We're going to meet in his cabin once the ship is under sail.'

That operation was already going ahead. The ship had been set on her course eastwards, and there was no need for further warping by the small boats. The rigging was full of seamen unfurling the sails, and below the deck-hands waited alertly by the braces, sheets, and falls. Like the unfolding of great white lilies the top-sails on the fore- and mainmasts spread out vastly to take without protest the faint breeze. The foresail and mizzen followed, and the last hawser on the stern was cast off.

More cheers went up. The *Wasa* was under way, but being still in waters sheltered by the high cliffs of Söder, and with only four of her sails set, her pace did not increase enough to cause any but the smallest rowing-boats in her escort to fall back. Little more than deep ripples went swishing back from the swan-like bow.

With everybody else Jacintha clapped her hands over her ears as two of the *Wasa*'s guns went booming forth to signal departure, and so quiet was the air that the acrid smoke lingered in blue-grey wisps smudging a sea that was rose and gold under the evening sky.

'Hans will be going below to meet me now,' Lysbeth said, and darted away. Then suddenly it came to Jacintha where she might find Axel, and she followed her sister, but took the companionway leading up into the afterpart. There was no one about. All were on deck, or on duty elsewhere. Lighted lanthorns illumined the carvings not reached by the prism sunlight shining through the glazed windows that made up part of the gallery. Under one of them Axel was studying the mermaid caryatid.

He sensed that someone had paused close by, but thought it to be another interested in the ship's ornamentation, but for a less personal reason than his own. But then he glanced over his shoulder, and saw Jacintha in the shadows. His face tautened and set in wonderment at her presence, although he believed at that moment it was only reconsideration of his request that she should come aboard which had brought her to his side.

'The carver of this mermaid didn't do justice to you, Jacintha.' His voice was thick with the pleasure that he was at a loss how to express, so moved was he that she was there. 'He has captured your beauty, but nothing of your heart.'

She stepped forward, and the light of the lanthorn fell full upon her face. He saw how she was looking at him, and was stunned to silence by it. Slowly he put out his hands to take hers and draw her close to him, and knew that they were meeting on individual crests of love—his deep-rooted and of long standing, and hers newly-found, tender, vulnerable, but uncompromising in its abandonment. His gaze was entranced.

'I love you, Axel,' she said in clear low tones. 'It has taken me a long time to realize that there are some loves—however sweet—that must be allowed to fade with the past. Perhaps until this day I was less mature than I had supposed myself to be. I've come to tell you now that I'm to bear your child, and he shall grow up at Halvarsensgaard just as you did, and all those generations before you.'

Then, when he still made no move, spoke no word, she flung her arms about his neck with passionate violence, kissing him with a fury that made him crush her tight, and together they

250

clung and swayed, lost in loving, oblivious of all else except their joy and rapture in each other.

It was the sharp listing of the floor beneath their feet that broke their embrace, and sent them tumbling down together. Cries of surprise and alarm came echoing from other parts of the ship, and there was a rumble as a one-pounder, the only gun-tackle that had not been pulled taut and belayed, went crashing and bouncing across the maindeck.

'God's wounds! What's amiss?' Axel exclaimed grimly as he caught her up, and they staggered together again as the ship righted herself, making the dancing lanthorns cast their swinging lights even more wildly over the beams and the bulkheads. He hurried her back towards the deck, although the ship was sailing as smoothly as before.

Outside in the sun all the visitors were laughing and talking with the embarrassed fervour of those caught off-guard and alarmed by a perfectly commonplace incident. Only the seamen exchanged puzzled glances, and looked up at the sails that had filled so briefly with a sudden rush of wind that had swept like a released draught from the distant heights of the Söder cliffs.

'The *Wasa* has been floated with too much wine,' Axel joked lightly to reassure Jacintha, who was staring up into his face, seeing the gravity that lay behind his eyes, and she continued to cling to him, careless of any who might stare in their direction. 'No doubt she will soon steady herself,' he continued more seriously. 'The Captain has to learn the little whims and ways of his new mistress before he can master her to his satisfaction.'

Jacintha's deep gaze on him did not falter, and he saw that she was not to be decieved as to the conviction that he harboured that the *Wasa* would not be able to weather a squall or a storm. He folded his arms about her shoulders, and put his lips to her forehead.

Then again there came a sudden lurch to port as a gust of wind filled the sails, stronger this time, for the *Wasa* was moving to a point where the land fell back. Axel made a grasp for a rope, using all his strength as he held Jacintha to him, bracing his feet against the gunwale as the deck listed away from them again, sending screaming and shouting passengers, soldiers, and those of the crew who had not leapt for the rigging or some other hand-hold, sliding and falling about. Again the one-pounder went thumping across, its bronze dolphins flashing back the evening sun-light, knocking from under them the feet of several people that had managed to keep their balance.

Down, down, down went the deck. On the lower battery deck a number of gunners were on duty, lounging about their 24-pounders as they talked together, but suddenly the conversation of those on the port side died away, and all stared as the water, swirling glittering bubbles to the very lip of the open gun-ports, lapped the edges, and then gently receded again.

One man gave a low alarmed whistle through his teeth. 'Did yer see that? Someone 'ad better get an officer down 'ere, and sharp! The weight of the cannon must be trimmed!'

In his cabin leading from the upper battery deck Hans was trying to comfort the weeping Lysbeth, who—now that the hour of parting had drawn so near, and the excitement of coming aboard subsided—did not know how she could endure a separation of months, and perhaps even a year or more, from this husband and lover so dear to her.

'I cannot bear it,' she had declared over and over again.

If Hans had been less preoccupied in swearing his undying love, making wild promises of a speedy return, he might have paid more attention to the wide listing of the ship. But although the disciplined part of his mind was registering that all was not as it should be, he knew that once on deck again there would be no more private moments with his wife, and he could not bring himself to leave her in her great distress to see what was going on up aloft. He spun about and yanked open the door in irritation when a hasty knocking came upon it,

253

and glared ferociously at the young gunner who stood there.

'What is it?' he snapped. 'Up to the lower gun-ports? Very well. I'll come down. Return to your post.' He was about to follow the gunner immediately, aware of the urgency of investigating the matter, but as he threw a backward look over his shoulder at Lysbeth she snatched at him, trying to hold him back.

'Don't leave me yet!' she wailed despairingly.

'I must go!' He tried to disentangle her hands, but she buried her face against him, her sobs becoming noisy. 'Come with me then,' he said in desperation, and was aware of the amused glances of the seamen as he led her with him down to the deck below.

There had been just as much confusion on the maindeck when the ship righted itself once more as there had been during the listing. Those already floundering about on the boards were sent sliding back again amid renewed screaming and the high shrill wailing of frightened children. Captain Hansson's voice came booming through his speaking trumpet as he ordered the casting loose of the topsails, but the wind had gone down again, the air as still as before, and in spite of being well-greased, the ropes were stiff and inflexible in their newness, and the deckhands sweated to get them through the blocks.

Jacintha fell back a step from Axel as he

released her, resting the flat of her hands against her aching rib-cage that he had gripped so tightly to keep her from falling. 'I declare this ship rocks like a cradle,' she managed to say with a smile, but her eyes were sombre. All around them people were getting to their feet again, anxious and shaken, some of the women weeping as they hugged their children close, and pleaded to be put ashore.

'Can you swim?' he asked quietly, looking at her under his lashes. She nodded, and his face relaxed into grin. 'God's mercy! To think I've known everything else about you except that.' He put out his hands and unclasped her cloak, brushing her chin with an affectionate finger as he did so. 'Just in case—'

His words were cut short as a whirling gust sent the great sails thundering, the flags snapping at the mastheads, and the ship heeled over hard to port. On the lower battery deck water gushed through the open gun-ports. Too late Axel had grabbed for Jacintha. Although he caught her shoulder, the loosened cloak slipped in his hand, and he saw her go flying away from him. Then he himself went whirling like a top, crashing into others. He scrambled to his feet, but could not see her. There was no righting of the deck this time. The ship was already sinking.

He tried to thrust his way through the screaming, panic-stricken crowd, helping up those in his path, shouting to the men to kick off their boots, the women to discard their petticoats, but in the noise it was doubtful if any heard him. Then, screwing up his eyes at the terrible sight, he saw a shining skim of green water rise above the port gunwale. It seemed almost to stretch, and then it broke, pouring galloping foam with a roar into the waist of the ship.

Below Lysbeth and Hans would have been trapped in the flooded lower battery deck if the gunners, wary of the next list, had not shouted a warning, and bolted themselves to safety. Even so, the young couple had been up to their armpits in water by the time they reached the companionway, and it had been only the force of the invoked current bearing them towards it that had enabled Hans to reach out and seize the wooden slat.

Hysterical with fear, Lysbeth crawled on to the upper battery deck, and stumbled to her feet as Hans clambered from the companionway at the very moment that the water seized it from under his feet and sent it swirling away.

'Up the next one!' he shouted, hustling her towards the hatch where the widely slanting rays of the sun showed the way for gunners and seamen scrambling up it. Lysbeth, thrust forward to join in the rush for safety, found her foot so entangled in her dripping skirts that she could not mount, blocking the way. As though in unspoken agreement both Hans and a seaman took handfuls of her gown, and ripped it from her, taking her petticoats with it. In her lace-trimmed shift she was bundled up to the main deck with Hans close behind her. At that moment the *Wasa* capsized completely with a slow and awful grace.

Those watching from the little bobbing boats all around saw the sails cut into the water, and the pennants on the mast tops fluttered gaily until that moment when they were lost from sight for ever. The whole catastrophe had taken a matter of minutes. The *Wasa*, pride of the Royal Fleet, went slowly down to the bottom of the sea.

Nothing remained except a flotsam of odd pieces of wood and cork, and in between men, women, and children splashed and struggled to keep afloat, their cries of help resounding pitifully in the clear air. The rescuers, stunned and shocked by the disaster they had viewed on that quiet Sunday evening, worked frantically, pulling one half-drowned person after another into their boats. They were joined almost at once by other helpers, who—having witnessed the tragedy from the shore—had put out with their own fishing-boats and sailing craft.

It was a bulky florid-faced farmer in his best church-going clothes who lifted Jacintha into his boat, and she collapsed in a pool of her own sodden skirts, coughing and gasping, a hand to her throat, her dripping hair hanging over her face. Then she raised her head, and looked with strained, red-rimmed eyes towards the other boats in the hope that she would see Axel. Others were helped aboard, and when it was so crowded that the farmer did not dare to take on another person, he pulled for shore. There willing hands helped them out, and those too exhausted to walk were carried up the grassy slope towards the cottages. Kindly women were waiting with blankets and shawls that they threw around the survivors' shoulders, and Jacintha found herself enveloped in a cape of sheep-skin.

But she did not rest as they wanted her to. She went plodding amongst those who had been brought ashore, looking for only one face. Her mind registered that Hans and Lysbeth were there, kneeling and facing each other in the grass, arms about each other, like reunited children, but she did not pause to speak to them. There was only one purpose in her mind. Axel. Axel. Axel. Her heart cried his name.

She was vaguely aware that there was something familiar in the way she kept the sheepskin cape huddled about her, trailing it over rocks and through the grass that was a-shimmer with harebells. Then she rememberd the fox-quilt that she had kept around her when she had run downstairs at Halvarsensgaard to call to him in the snow.

And there he was. Stepping with bowed shoulders out of another boat just unloading at a little jetty below. She felt the tears of joy start from her eyes.

'Axel!' she called exultantly.

His tired head jerked up, and his face broke into a wonderful smile of love and relief and thankfulness. She began to run down to him, letting the cape go, and he rushed to meet her, his arms outstretched. As they met he swept her up and around, and then hugged her close, his mouth lost in hers. And it seemed to her that every harebell rang with the sweetest chime she had ever heard.

Photoset, printed and bound in Great Britain by
REDWOOD BURN LIMITED, Trowbridge, Wiltshire